ABOUT THIS BOOK

Mocked, ridiculed, and sentenced to death, seven-year-old River is saved from the noose when the Sisters McNee find her. They take her to their home in Havenwood Falls, a place for people like her to live safely, without fear of persecution. But what if the threat to their safety is River herself?

Her fire-maiden origins are a mystery. One a child has no hope of explaining. Then one futuristic vision from a well-respected member of the community seals her fate.

Flames.

Chaos.

Complete destruction.

Sixteen years later, River has come of age in the era of prosperity, prohibition, and ragtime music—and even as an adult, she still hates her power, resolute to never use it again. She tries to stay under the radar, but there is no hiding from the penetrating eyes of Jonas Pederson. Despite repeated warnings that she is dangerous, he won't stop pursuing her until she understands that he can easily survive her flames—even if he needs to show her his own well-protected secret.

It might be too late for River, though, when a threat from the past ignites that horrible vision.

Flames.

Chaos.

Destruction.

In the end, it will all be ashes.

LEGENDS OF HAVENWOOD FALLS BOOKS

Also try the main Havenwood Falls series; the YA line, Havenwood Falls High; the darker, sexier side of town, Havenwood Falls Sin & Silk; and the local supernatural college, Sun & Moon Academy.

Stay up to date at www.HavenwoodFalls.com

ALSO BY DESIREE LAFAWN

CONTEMPORARY ROMANCE

The Permanence of Pain

Beck the Halls – A Gallery B Christmas

GLASS CITY HEARTS

Gabe (Book One)

Dino (Book Two)

Jesse (Book Three)

PARANORMAL ROMANCE

Havenwood Falls Short Story Anthology 2018

Kiss the Ashes (A Legends of Havenwood Falls Novella)

Shiny Dancer: Mountain Mermaids (Sapphire Lake)

KISS THE ASHES

A LEGENDS OF HAVENWOOD FALLS NOVELLA

DESIREE LAFAWN

A sincere thank you to every reader that loses yourself in these pages. I hope you enjoy this glimpse into the past of Havenwood Falls, and it leaves you curious for the future. This book, and every book I write, is for you.

Fear not for the future, weep not for the past.
—Percy Bysshe Shelley

CHAPTER 1

RIVER

SUMMER 1908, CARLISLE, PENNSYLVANIA

I would never get used to hard-soled shoes even as an adult, but as a girl of seven I hated them. I'd much rather have gone barefoot, but the teachers in Carlisle were adamant the children properly dress themselves at all times. Dressed according to their standards, anyway. Our parents stood opposed even as the soldiers dragged us from the reservation.

"Who are you to take our children?" they cried out, unable to do more than shake their fists and stomp their feet; our once proud nation reduced to servants of a government foreign to us. A government so hell-bent on erasing our existence they uprooted the native children and forced them into boarding schools to learn the English way. Eliminate the savages and teach the children to be productive members of society.

Kill the Indian. Save the man.

Even now, many years later and grown, I have trouble wrapping my mind around the thought process that led to the exodus of the children—the reeducation process. But that had happened. And the history books will more than likely gloss it over the more time marches

1

on, but I will never forget being five years old and plucked from the small plot of land I considered my home.

Parents wept.

But not my parents. They died of the great sickness a year before. I had no parents to hold me in their arms as the soldiers came and separated us. No one fought for me, so when the time came to leave— aside from dragging my heels in the dirt—nothing stopped the soldiers from putting me on the wagon, squeezing me up against the rows of other crying, terrified children.

But I was different. If they knew how different, would they have placed me with the other children? Would they have taken me? There was no way to know, and I wouldn't explain because I had learned long ago that *my* kind of different was best kept hidden. Even from my own people.

So to the Carlisle Indian Industrial School I went, sandwiched in with many other children from mixed tribes, all learning to speak English and change everything about themselves. The administration beat the students who cried, and the angry, rebellious ones received a harsher punishment. One so severe, we feared talking about it amongst ourselves—because those students left without warning and didn't come back. But I didn't cry, and I didn't rebel. I obeyed, because I knew no other way. And there I lived for two years, suffering at the hands of my oppressors under the guise of spiritual cleansing until the summer of my seventh year.

I made a mistake.

It was playtime in the yard. That short time of day between morning chores and evening chores when there was a small sliver of space to remember that we were just children. It was my favorite time, and every chance I thought I could get away with it, I'd chuck my shoes under the shade of a white oak tree and curl my toes in the grass. Not running, not moving, just standing in place, anchored to the earth. Eyes closed, I stood under the tree with my arms raised out to the sides, feeling the wind above and below me.

The Great Thunder is near, I thought to myself, smelling the rain on the wind. *I wonder what mischief the Thunder Boys will be up to tonight.* The Great Thunder and his sons were a myth, and I dared not speak of it out loud, not when the teachers could hear. Speaking the stories of my people was forbidden and the punishment severe. But since no one controlled what went on in my head, I would think as I pleased.

"Come back here, Thomas," a voice shouted angrily, interrupting my peaceful moment. "You've stolen the bread; we know you have. Come receive your punishment."

A small brown blur came running across the packed dirt yard, and children of various ages stopped mid-play to see the boy running with the bit of bread locked in his fist. He came to a screeching halt about fifteen feet from where I stood, under my oak tree, and facing off like a boxer, he scowled at his aggressor.

I recognized the boy from my old village. I remembered when his mother had clung to him and the soldiers yanked him, only a year younger than myself, from her grieving arms. They'd given him a new name when he'd come to this school, just as they'd done me, but I knew his real name was Wesa. I knew because his mother had screamed it to the sky as they had taken away the children.

Wesa. Two years he'd been here, knowing the rules. And still he stole the bread.

Oh, Wesa, what will happen to you now?

Thomas now, no longer Wesa, stood in front of the man who'd been so aggressively calling his name. His cotton button-down shirt had come untucked from his plain brown breeches while chasing the boy, and he stood, panting, mouth drawn down in a formidable frown.

"Thomas. You've stolen food. Accept the punishment." The man's expression was stern, his eyes hard and unfeeling.

Wesa fidgeted before opening his hand to show the small bit of bread clutched in his fist. "But I'm so hungry, Mr. Crane." He looked at the food, his eyes wet and his lower lip trembling. "Please, I didn't want to steal, but I'm so hungry."

Sorrow gripped my heart for him. My stomach often felt hollow from the slim allotment of rations we were each given per day. And he was so young. *Poor Wesa.* Mr. Crane's features relaxed, and I breathed an inaudible sigh of relief. Mr. Crane was not a very nice man by nature, but I'd never *seen* him hurt any of the students. The same couldn't be said for other teachers. Several of them seemed to only be working at the boarding school because they loved tormenting children, seeking reasons to dole out discipline.

Mr. Crane just always had a sour look on his face, and even though he always smelled like whiskey, I'd never seen him raise his hand in anger.

"Bring it, Thomas." Mr. Crane raised his hand and beckoned Thomas closer. Two tears snaked down the small boy's cheeks, but the will of the older man won, and the younger of the two made slow shuffling steps across the packed dirt of the yard, head hanging low in defeat. Eyes so downcast he didn't see the blow coming and didn't even get to react. My seven-year-old self could do nothing but watch openmouthed at the violence that unfolded.

The cuff on the side of his six-year-old head lifted him straight off the ground and onto his back where he lay, a sad pile of arms and legs in the dirt.

"Thieves are beaten, Thomas," Mr. Crane said calmly, standing over the small boy on the ground too stunned to even react as the older man plucked the bread from his now slack grip. He grimaced and crumbled the small loaf with one hand until it was nothing but crumbs drifting to the ground. I mourned the loss of the food myself, hand drifting to my empty stomach. Now no one would get to eat it.

"If we let you do it, then everyone would think it entitled them to more than we give them, boy. You aren't special. None of you are. But if you're so hungry, you can eat your bread in the mud like an animal. Are you an animal, Thomas?" Mr. Crane's face twisted into something monstrous, and he stepped on the small pile of bread crumbs with his dusty brown shoe. "Go on, Thomas; eat it if you're hungry. This is good enough for you."

The small boy looked up from his place on the ground, afraid to move. More tears fell down his face, his little shoulders shaking with fear—or pain—maybe both. He made no move toward the pile in the dirt and crumbs, and still I stood in place, caught inside the vision

4

with no way out. Mr. Crane sneered at him, his eyes a window to the depths of an ugly soul. Without warning, Mr. Crane's leg shot out, and his dirty brown shoe connected with the small boy's legs, lifting him up a few inches and sending him spinning farther in the dirt. Wesa—or Thomas, as they called him—lay on his back, clutching his side and crying. He made no move to get to his feet.

The air no longer smelled of rain. Instead, the wind carried the scent of burning. Similar to that of the blaze we gathered around when we had our own land, where the warriors told the tales of the hunt and the women sang their songs and cooked the meat. It was the smell of the fatwood just sparking, smoky and warm but not yet blistering. It was a small fire, but with enough tending it would become a great blaze, hot enough to sear anything placed before it. The breeze tickled my skin and moved the stray hairs that stuck out of my braids around my face. I didn't know where the wind had come from, but it did nothing to cool the aching itch marching up and down my skin, nor the anger that was bubbling just below the surface.

Mr. Crane was hurting Wesa—and no one was doing a thing to stop it.

He was a small boy, not so different from myself, who was just hungry. We all were, and that was a fact, but he was only six and didn't have as much of a grasp of self-control, even after two years in their Anglo prison. But Mr. Crane would make an example out of him regardless. The older man bore down on the child, his face as red as his facial hair, a grim smile plastered on his face.

He's happy. My inner thoughts echoed the stark reality. Even as a young child, I still understood. *He wants to hurt Wesa.*

But Wesa was so small, he couldn't take much more. Still no one in the yard moved. All those small faces looked on with fear in their eyes. No one would stand up for Wesa; no one could. Everyone knew what the punishment for rebellion was. I had seen the stone markings before —set up in the woods a short bit away from the school. That's where rebellion led you—to your very own stone marking in the dirt.

But even so, watching Mr. Crane as he reached the spot where he had kicked the young boy and hauled him back to his feet by his close-cropped hair had me gritting my teeth, the taste of bile and ash in my throat. He cocked back his fist and hit Wesa once; the impact split the skin on his chin and blood spurted out. Wesa cried. The smoke in the air stung my eyes, and my voice was that of a stranger croaking out of a throat lined with rocks and silt.

"No."

I wasn't loud enough. Mr. Crane didn't hear me, or at least pretended he didn't as he shook the boy until his feet left the ground, and he hung there in his master's hands, limp as an animal removed from a trap. "Come, Thomas, to punishment with you."

To punishment. As if the six-year-old hadn't been through enough. There was nowhere that Mr. Crane would take him that could be any improvement, and I doubted Wesa could even walk by himself. Blood poured from that angry cut on his face, and the crimson trail dripping from his tiny chin matched the hue of my blistering rage.

I found my voice.

"No." The heated breeze carried the word farther this time. This time Mr. Crane heard me, and his head snapped up, his eyes zeroing in on me from where he stood a short distance away. His mouth dropped open, but he didn't release his hold on the small boy.

"Mary, what are you doing?" *Mary.* That was my new name. I wasn't supposed to think of myself as River anymore, but sometimes I forgot. Times like now, when the atrocity I had just witnessed placed me somewhere outside of myself—outside of my safety nets and away from right and wrong.

I was just so *angry*.

Uncertainty graced Mr. Crane's face, and he took a small step back. I didn't want him to take a step back. I wanted him to let go of Wesa.

"No. You let him go. You hurt him—you're a bad man." The air snapped and crackled around me, and my braids rose and fell in this new heated breeze before unraveling completely. My long tresses danced in the angry wind.

"What are you doing?" the older man whispered, his eyes no

longer narrow and cruel, but wide and fearful. "What are you—? Stay back. Stay away—"

But I didn't stay away. I couldn't, because Mr. Crane still had his meaty hand fisted in Wesa's short dark hair and was dragging him backward across the ground. Rage burned in my belly. He was a bad man. He hurt Wesa. He needed to be punished.

The ground I stood on cracked beneath my feet, the air so hot, the dirt released what little moisture it had and hardened like wood. The small bit of grass I'd curled my toes in earlier incinerated as if it had never been. I barely noticed. The heat. The smell. The acidic swell burning and churning deep in my belly—all were secondary to my rage as I looked at the man who had beaten a small boy to near unconsciousness.

"Drop him." The words blasted out of my mouth with ferocity, and Mr. Crane complied without thinking. Wesa just lay there, crumpled where he fell. The only movement in the entire yard was the myriad of small heads swiveling to look from Mr. Crane to me. The same look of horror that had been focused on Mr. Crane now moved to me. I didn't care.

I couldn't see any of them anymore. All I could see was the form of the man in front of me, the one who had such blackness in his soul, he could beat a child with a smile on his face. I only had eyes for him. Two other teachers had come into the yard by now—Mr. Weisman and Mrs. Crane. They had come out to see what was going on, I was sure, but I couldn't count on either of them to help in this situation. No, I'd witnessed their punishments before. No help would come from any of the adults in this building. I'd need to take care of them myself.

"What on earth is going on out here? Oh—" Mrs. Crane's sentence ended in a bloodcurdling shriek. "Mary! It's witchcraft! Savage witchcraft!"

I ignored her. I was far too focused on the backward steps of Mr. Crane as he tried to put as much space between the two of us as possible. Mr. Weisman had no such sense of self-preservation, and he marched to where I stood, circumventing Wesa on the ground as if he was nothing more than a puddle of dirty water. He almost made it in time to stop me. Almost.

I felt the graze of his fingers on my arm before I opened my mouth to scream. Dry, cracked lips pulled back as far as I was able, but no sound escaped. I spoke no words because I had none to give. But I had something else. That which I had been hiding for as long as I could remember. That twisting ache in my guts I had spent years learning to ignore, or at least keep hidden from everyone around me. My parents had taught me that, if not much else. Hide it away or bad things would happen.

Well, I'd hidden it all this time, and bad things still happened. There was no need to hide it anymore, so I let the mangled ropes of burning fury snake their way out of the depths of my body and erupt from my mouth in a single blast of heat and flame. I might not have any words to exorcise my rage, but I did have my fire.

CHAPTER 2

RIVER

*A*s a child I'd never thought of killing anyone before. I'd seen dead people, but I'd never inflicted damage on another human soul intending to end their life. But with Mr. Crane lying in a pile on the charred ground in front of me, I was having trouble dredging up any regret about what I had done.

Especially when I could still see the little ball of crying boy on the ground just a little farther away.

Mr. Crane was a bad man.

He also wasn't dead. The fire had spewed forth from my belly angry and hot, but it had done little damage besides heating the air and charring his hair and clothes. He threw himself on the ground in what was probably a mixture of self-preservation and fear, and had smothered the flames most likely without even thinking about it.

I'd acted without thinking, as most children do, but my actions still had the desired effect. Mr. Crane had stopped hurting Wesa. I'd not thought a single second past that goal, and I wasn't prepared to defend myself as the hands of the other adults in the yard descended on my seven-year-old self, slinging me over a meaty shoulder by my legs as my hair hung down over my face, obscuring my vision.

"Get her out of here, Hank," Mrs. Crane squawked as Mr. Weisman carted me out of the yard at a run. "I don't know what dirty little trick she pulled, but she won't get another chance. Lock her away until we decide on her punishment. Get up, Yancy," she leveled at Mr. Crane where he still lay on the ground. "You've been had by the tricks of a child. You're an embarrassment to everyone."

She may have had more to say, but Mr. Weisman carried me too far to hear, and I couldn't see through the hair that hung down over my face. He carried me far enough that the blood rushing to my head obliterated any sound at all, and I had trouble getting my bearings as I was suddenly righted and sat down on an upside-down crate in a dark room I'd never been in before.

With my hair now out of my face and the blood that had been thundering in my head receding, I could see the face of Mr. Weisman as he towered above me.

"I'm afraid you've stepped in something you can't step out of, Mary girl." He sighed and scrubbed his hands over his face. I didn't want to think about what he meant, but I couldn't help but notice I was in an old storeroom out back, away from other people, and not back in the dormitory to await a normal punishment like I had thought I would be. "I know you thought you were helping Thomas, but it will only be worse for you now, you know? Not sure what they'll do with you, but it can't be good from the look of things. You attacked a teacher. They'll nip that right away, I'm sure."

I said nothing, just looked up at Mr. Weisman, trying not to let the fear I felt show on my face. I'd learned long ago to hide the things that were strange about me. To swallow it down and not let it out. It wasn't just strangers and those at the school who would persecute me if they knew. My own people were not immune to fear either. My parents had taught me long ago that the world was a dangerous place, and I knew the cost of letting my power show.

But my parents died, and I'd revealed my secret.

Not a single soul in this world would help me now.

"Hold out your hands, then, Mary," Mr. Weisman said as he pulled a heavy cord from a hook on the wall. Willing my arms not to shake, I did as he asked. "Now Michelle thinks you pulled some trick on Yancy to get him to leave Thomas alone, but I was there. I know what I saw. Even now I see—your eyes are straight black, all the way through. Just a little bit of the white showing on the outside now, when there was none earlier. That's not normal, girl." He continued to speak as he wound the corded rope around my wrists, binding my hands together in front of me. I didn't know what to say to him. I'd only used my fire once before, and only in front of my parents, so I didn't know my eyes changed colors at all.

"I know you're something different. I've met others like you before. Well, not exactly like you. I don't know what you are," he said as he cut off the trailing ends of rope and patted my knee where I sat. "Once met a man who could tell things would happen before they did. Knew a lady that could tell what you were thinking when the words hadn't even left your mouth yet. You're someone like them, I suppose, although that was a pitiful display back there." Stepping away from me and walking toward the door, he paused, his back to me. "I hope it was worth it, Mary. You might have gotten the eyes off young Thomas, but now they're all on you. Lord knows what they're going to do with you now. That Michelle—she doesn't have a compassionate bone in her body. It's a damn shame, it is, but you called her attention on you now."

So he was one of *those* kind, then. I'd met people like Hank Weisman before. People who didn't like the hard-hearted things they saw going on around them, but did nothing to fix them. It wasn't that he wanted to tie me up—he didn't want anything bad to happen to me. He just didn't care enough to help me, even though he knew it would be bad. I hoped that when I died, as I was going to, I could come back to the earth in another time period, when the world wasn't full of so many evil people and cowards.

If everyone was just a little bit braver, we could change the world.

Taking my silence as acceptance, Mr. Weisman opened the door to leave, letting a tiny sliver of sunlight in through the open door, illuminating the rest of the room I was being held in. It was a storage room—mostly extra wood and tools—as well as drums of oil for lamps stacked in a corner.

"You'll need to sit tight for a while, Miss Mary, until she comes for you. I wouldn't try any of your fancy smoke effects either—I doubt even you would survive the explosion if you breathe hot in here." And with that, he shut me in, locking the door behind him and eliminating the only light in the entire room.

I didn't know if I would survive or not. I didn't know a single thing about my power to produce fire besides the fact that I could do it at all. It wasn't something that had passed from my parents, that was for sure. No one knew what I was, or what I was capable of; we only knew to suppress it so no one would find out. And this was why. I may have saved Wesa temporarily, but I had doomed myself instead. It terrified my seven-year-old self, and I cried in the dark, knowing there would be no one to let me out even if I made enough noise to be heard.

AFTER AN UNDETERMINED AMOUNT of time sitting on the edge of the crate with my bound hands in my lap, my back cramping and complaining, I slid to the floor and rested my back against the wood. I must have rested my eyes as well, because they popped open with a start when the storage room door opened. No daylight streamed in through the doorway this time, so I guessed they had confined me for half a day at least, as it was full night. The soft light of an oil lantern flickered in the doorway for an instant, and then I saw nothing but blackness as a heavy sack was pulled tight over my head and they lifted me to my feet.

I thought I'd been afraid when the soldiers had come and rounded up the children to go to that school in the first place. I knew nothing then. Crying in the solitude of the darkened storage shed, with my hands bound in front of me and my legs shaking with dread, I'd been woefully unprepared. For no other experience in my life compared to the absolute terror of having my eyes covered and my body slung over the shoulder of a man who wasn't Mr. Weisman this time.

The smell of whiskey filled my nose, and it wasn't until they dumped me into the back of a wagon and the horse moved that I understood who had taken me.

"You're drunk, Yancy. Can you even see to steer the horse? Move aside. Give me the reins." That was the voice of Mrs. Crane for sure. I didn't know where we were going, but I could tell by the way my little body bumped and rolled around in the cart it was uneven ground, and by the length of time we traveled, I imagined we were quite a way from the school.

It's a terrifying thing for any adult—that moment of realization when they know *without a shred of doubt* they are living their last moments. But for me, as a child who'd only known the fear of hiding my entire life, it was a different feeling. The rough fibers of fraying rope digging into the sensitive skin over my collarbone and the dark canvas bag that had been slapped over my head just seemed like the obvious ending to my short, pitiful story.

This wasn't punishment. This was death. I deserved this end, and I didn't belong here.

They never took the bag off my head, not even for a moment. Not when they slid me feet first off the wagon and made me walk behind them, my hands still bound in front of me and someone, probably Mr. Crane, leading by the rope already tied around my neck. I stumbled once, and the rope pulled tight, cutting my airway closed. Was this what it would be like to die? I didn't want it. Panic bloomed in my chest, and I cried, my sobs fighting to be free from my already restricted throat.

"It's too late for that, you little witch," Mrs. Crane hissed in my ear. "Every opportunity we've given you to become a good Christian, and you resort to filthy heathen ways."

"Attacked me, she did," Mr. Crane hiccupped from somewhere in front of me. "Burned the whiskers right off my chin. Can't let that go. One bad apple, you know, Michelle?"

"Yes, Yancy, I know. You have to cull the herd to keep the sheep in line. We won't suffer troublemakers, Mary."

I wanted to yell and scream. I wanted to tell them my name wasn't Mary, but I couldn't say a word. That rope cutting the air from my lungs, even just briefly, froze my entire body. Any amount of energy I had left was focusing on moving one foot in front of the other in a straight line, so I didn't stumble again.

Then we stopped walking, and no one spoke again for quite some time. The silence was just as unnerving as when they were talking. There were the light sounds of people at work, like the Cranes were setting up whatever they would do, and I was left to stand by a tree with my hands still tied in front of me and the rough bark scraping against my back. It was difficult to breathe inside the sack on my head, but after that tiny taste of suffocation, any breaths were a luxury.

I thought I'd imagined it—a shuffling behind the tree I was standing against, a quiet whispering through the tall grass that tickled my shins. But it continued, and as I strained my ears to catch the sounds that the Cranes were too busy to notice, a small voice carried through the air next to my head, as if coming from my mind itself.

"Little girl," it whispered. "Don't make a sound, but if you can hear me, tap your foot two times." I was sure I was crazy. A disembodied voice in the woods. Talking to me. And only I could hear it? Maybe I was going insane before they put me to death. I was too young to know any better.

"Sister, you have to be more specific. Maybe she doesn't understand what you mean?" A different yet similar voice to the first floated by my other ear.

"Will you be quiet and let me work? I'm trying not to scare her, and you're jabbering away."

"Sister, just tell her we'll help her. If she knows, she'll be able to handle the after parts."

"You're right, sister," the first voice replied. "We will help you, dear. If you understand that, can you tap your left foot two times? It doesn't have to be a big tap; we'll be able to see it."

I tapped my left foot two times softly in the grass. I could hear the Cranes moving around in the near distance, somehow missing the entire exchange. I did not understand what was going on, but the strange voices whispering were the friendliest I'd heard in ages, so I listened.

"Okay now, dear, just do what they want you to do and don't be afraid anymore. It will get loud . . ."

"It's going to sound like the hounds of hell are coming for their souls, if we play our cards right," the other voice interrupted, still barely a thought on the breeze, "but it should get their britches in a twist enough for us to steal you away."

"Yes, thank you, sister," the first voice chided. "We'll be stealing you away, is that all right?" For what purpose they would be stealing me for I didn't know, but it couldn't be as bad as dying at the end of a dirty rope, so I nodded my head slightly, and the voice continued. "It will be loud, dear, and I'm sorry ahead of time for that, but you can't move, okay? Act like you don't hear it at all."

And then the voices disappeared, and I felt the slack on the rope tighten as the Cranes finished whatever prep work had kept them busy for the last few minutes. I wasn't sure what would happen, but hope swelled in my small chest as I gave myself over to the possibility I might just get saved.

CHAPTER 3

RIVER

*E*ven with advance notice, I wasn't prepared for the horrifying sound. It started with footsteps, running through the grass on all sides of me; one going from right to left, and one going from left to right. That canvas bag was still over my head, but my covered eyes just made my ears that much sharper, and I could just about hear the grass blades bending as they circled our little patch.

"What in the hell is that?" Mr. Crane bellowed.

"Who's out there?" Mrs. Crane whimpered, letting me know the two voices had moved but still could not be seen.

"It's probably just animals, badger maybe, or raccoons."

"Yancy, I don't think raccoons move that fast, do they?"

"How the hell should I know, woman?" Mr. Crane mumbled irritably. "Just get her strung up, kick the stool, and let's go."

So that was how it was to be then? They would prop me up, tie my rope off and then let me swing until I was dead? Those heartless people. A little less afraid now I knew someone was in my corner, I could only find sadness in my heart for how hateful they were.

And then the wailing started.

A ghastly moaning started low, rising in pitch until it hit a full crescendo of keening sobs. Cries. Phantom noises seemed to come from everywhere, and still nowhere. The shivers started in my toes and ran up, marching like insects from the soles of my feet up and out through the top of my head, but I willed my body not to move. I acted like I didn't hear a thing.

Mrs. Crane screamed. So did Mr. Crane, and the noises sounded shockingly similar to each other.

Still, I didn't move.

The wailing continued. If anything, it grew louder and more concentrated, closer even, until it sounded like the source was two inches in front of my face even though I couldn't see through the bag on my head.

"It's fairies!" shrieked a terrified Mrs. Crane. "She's called fairies, and they will steal us away."

"Shut up, Michelle," Mr. Crane bellowed, and I felt slack in the rope hanging around my neck. "Get on the buggy, and let's get out of here."

"But the girl—"

"Let the fairies take her then. Are you so ignorant you want to hang around and go with them?"

And the wailing continued. On and on it went for an undetermined amount of time while I heard a whip crack and answering neighs as the horse thundered off at a fast clip. My ears picked up the sound of wagon wheels bouncing on the dirt and then . . . nothing.

The noise halted as if a door shut on it, and even the normal night noises ceased to exist in the wake of that performance. And yet still I didn't move. I acted like I heard nothing and knew nothing, just as the two voices had instructed me to. I remained as still as a stone until someone whipped the bag off my head, and I stumbled against the tree I'd been standing against with a shriek.

Two gray heads popped into my field of vision. The faces on those heads were smiling kindly—the kind of smiles that reached their eyes —and their faces were lined with time and experience.

"Hullo," said one of the gray-haired ladies.

"Hullo," chimed in the other.

I stood there, still trussed with a rope hanging around my neck, its tail end lying in the dirt.

"Are you really fairies?" I whispered. I didn't know what *fairies* were, but these old women weren't so scary.

"Pfft," one of the gray-haired ladies sputtered, and the other smiled wide, showing a row of white, even teeth.

"Your version of fairies and ours are two different things, is what I think. You're probably thinking of sprites anyway. They're the wee buzzy ones with wings."

"Sister is right, and anyway, we're banshees. Didn't you hear the wailin'? No fairies I know can make a racket like that. Not that I've heard, anyway."

So they weren't fairies, but they had met some before? I didn't know what a fairy was; I'd only just heard the word from Mrs. Crane's screaming, so it was all news to me.

"I'm Meri," one woman said, laying her hand on the ropes that bound my hands. There was a gentle warmth, and the bindings fell away from me as if cut with an unseen knife. "That's my sister Alice."

As I turned my head to acknowledge the woman standing next to me, Meri placed her hands on my neck. After another brief warmth, the rope fell to the ground with a little plop in the dirt.

My little hands shook as I touched the raw marks where the rope had abraded my tender flesh. I'd felt death's breath on my skin, and these two had swooped in and saved me. I knew nothing more than that, but if they were here to spirit me away, I would go with them. These two kindly older women had given me more smiles and care in the last five minutes than I had been given in the last two years. I would follow them even if they didn't want me; that's how smitten I was in that moment.

"How did you know I was here?"

Alice looked at me shrewdly, assessing how much information she could give me, how much I could process in that moment, before she smiled again and nodded. "I had a dream about you, you see. Crying in the dark. Scared. You needed us, and we need you."

"You need me?" My voice was but a whisper. No one had needed me before. "But I'm not very good. I don't try to be bad, but . . ."

"Hush now," and before I knew it, Meri gathered me in the softest, warmest hug I had ever experienced. "You're not a bad girl, heavens no. You're just a wee bit different is all."

"You aren't a bad girl," Alice said from over my shoulder. "I dreamed of you. You're our girl, and if you're willing, we'll take you home with us."

"You want to take me with you?" I sniffed and peeked over Meri's shoulder at Alice, who winked at me and nodded.

"It's quite a journey from here, though," she said. "It'll probably take time. But when we get to where we're going, you'll finally have a safe place. There are lots of different people there. Like us, like yourself. Not exactly the same, but we're all special in our own ways. It's a safe place, girl."

I smiled at the thought. My life had been so dirty and ugly; a safe place seemed almost unimaginable.

Meri grumbled as I pulled out of her embrace during Alice's conversation. "What is your name? We can't just be on about calling you girl all the time. We've said ours—what are you called?"

"Wait!" Alice interrupted. "I dreamed it. I know. It's on the tip of my tongue and has something to do with water . . . its Stream isn't it?"

I giggled at her obviously wrong answer. Maybe her dreams weren't as clear as she thought.

"Raindrop," guessed Meri.

"Muddy Puddle!"

I dissolved in a fit of laughter at the last one when I figured out they were playing with me, and I realized it had been so long since I had laughed that I didn't even recognize the sound of my own.

"River, we've a long way to go before we're home," Alice said gently, taking one of my hands in hers as Meri took the other. "Are you ready to leave this all behind?"

I turned to look at the circle of forest for the first time since they had removed the bag. There were deep cuts in the earth where the wagon had sunk in and hoof prints all around. I looked up at the tree I had been destined to hang from, and down at the ground where my ropes lay like dead discarded snakes. Was I ready to leave this all behind?

I couldn't get away fast enough.

With the wide-eyed wonder of a child, I thought back to what the sisters had said about the wee fairies with wings.

"Are we going to fly to where we're going?" I asked in awe.

Meri regarded me thoughtfully. "That might require calling in a few favors I don't know we've earned as yet." She scratched her chin, and her eyes twinkled brightly. "I was thinking we'd take the train."

CHAPTER 4

JONAS

JUNE 1924, HAVENWOOD FALLS, COLORADO

*T*here were a lot of things to look forward to in life: birthdays, anniversaries, the weekend, and holidays. The thing I most looked forward to, however, was that daily noon bell. The four long blasts coming from the quarry rippled through the air like a punch, announcing to those of us working it was time to stop and eat.

Lunch break.

Not something to celebrate, at least not to the extent that I did, but it wasn't just the food I was looking forward to—it was the company. There were a lot of things I loved about Havenwood Falls after coming here as a lad of just sixteen, but my favorite by far was a certain someone that didn't even live within the town limits. I had to be content with those tiny stolen bits of company I was graced with, every day at noon.

The midday sun burned across my neck and back, through the work shirt to the white skin below. While I preferred the cool and dark inside the mine, I spent a lot of my time laboring in the sun. Being a mine worker was a hard job, but per my lineage, I was good at it. As cool as a Colorado mountain summer could be, even at seventy-one degrees my skin was flustered, prickly, and covered in a fine layer of grit.

It was to be expected, considering my line of work, but for a meeting with the most beautiful girl I had ever laid eyes on in all of my years on this earth, it wouldn't do. I picked the fabric of my shirt and pulled it away from my body, attempting to shake the dust and grime off as I walked up the steep hill to the place where the dirt and rock smoothed out into a wide grassy slope.

"It doesn't matter how you primp, she'll avoid you today just like she has every other day." The cheerful voice of Ian, my friend and fellow mine worker, sounded off behind me. "Is today the day you'll push past her defense? Or will you chicken out?"

"I don't chicken out," I said, as I shoved him in the arm. I didn't strike him hard at all, but I still felt a sense of satisfaction when he stumbled to the side a few feet before righting himself, grinning like a loon.

"I know you watch your strength around us tiny mortals," Ian mused, "but I think you might have maybe wanted to knock me down with that one."

"If I'd wanted you down, you'd be at the bottom of the mine by now." I returned his grin. He and I both knew I would never hurt him on purpose, just as we both knew no one in Havenwood Falls had ever seen my *real* strength. And that was all right. I was who I was and I wouldn't change that, but by nature, stone men weren't the most handsome of creatures, so I was very selective of those I showed my second self to. The girl I was trying to get to be mine was not on the short list.

"I will not chicken out, Ian." I smiled as we both crested the hill, stepped into the line where the dusty quarry rock met the grass, and scraped our dirty boots on the soft green carpet. "Today, I've a plan."

Ian's dark eyebrows rose in surprise, and his green eyes twinkled with mirth. "Oh, a plan, you have? Please share it with the rest of the class."

"I'm not telling you anything; now go have lunch with your fan club—I have a lady to woo."

Ian sputtered and coughed as he looked over his shoulder in the general direction I had been pointing. There was already a line of young ladies there, holding boxed lunches and drinks, presumably brought for their fathers and brothers, but I knew the truth. Their matchmaking mamas had sent them. Ian was an eligible young bachelor, and there was more than one way to net a husband.

"*My* fan club, you say?" Ian hissed under his breath. But I barely heard him, as I was already looking ahead, at the dark-haired young beauty who was bringing her motorcycle to a stop alongside the grassy area where we all gathered. A line was already forming in front of her, other men like me who ordered packed lunches from her cart every day. That was okay. I didn't need to be first in line—I needed to be last.

River McNee was the twenty-three-year-old adopted niece of the Sisters McNee, and she took orders for packed lunches and cold drinks from the laborers in town. Every day like a clock, she would bring those lunches in, collect our money, then ride that little motorbike with the side cart back out of town, and out of my life. I didn't like her for the lunches, although they were good enough in their own right. Sandwiches made with soft homemade bread piled high with— depending on the day—roast beef, salt ham, or thick slices of turkey meat. There was a crisp cold vegetable of some sort, and always, but always, a thick slice of pie. Whether River or the sisters was in charge of that pie, it was like magic in every bite. Peach, berry cobblers, apple —even when the fruit wasn't in season—the pie tasted like someone had plucked the fruit straight from the tree itself. That was the power of the pie.

But it still wasn't the reason I ordered lunch from that side cart every workday, without fail.

I watched as she chatted with everyone in line until it was my turn to address the young woman with the beautiful doe eyes and strangely colored hair. She kept it tied back in braids most often, but she couldn't hide the streaks of rust and flame that wove in and out no matter how tightly she bound it. Today she wore a short-sleeved dress the color of the bluebells that peppered the mountainside. It was plain, and the skirt hung damn near down to her ankles, but she still looked lovely to me. She tried to dress as modestly as she could, but there wasn't any amount of clothing aside from a winter parka that would hide the generous curve of those assets. Even now, as she smiled at me in greeting, the seams of her dress pulled tight in the front, and one little white button looked in dire need of saving. I imagined if she filled her lungs too deeply, it would come screaming off, pinging into the grass.

I wonder if I can get her to yell, I thought before giving myself a mental knock upside the head.

Don't disrespect her like that, you bastard, I told myself. *You're on a mission; remember your purpose.*

"What's the matter, Jonas? Is everything all right?"

It was that soft melodious voice, nothing more than a murmur really, that shook me from my perverse thoughts. I'd been inside my own head, and who knew how long I'd been standing in front of her, staring at her chest like a deviant without saying a word?

"W-what?" I hated that I stumbled over the word, but I wasn't sure if I had even heard her correctly. She was holding my sack lunch out, a bemused half smile on her face and her dark eyes laughing.

"You look so angry, what with your eyebrows all drawn together. I would have thought you didn't like your food, but you haven't even taken it from me yet." Then there was a flash of white as she smiled, a true smile that lit up her face, the grassy lawn we were standing in, and hell, half the town of Havenwood Falls. "And if it's cheering up you need, there's something in that bag that will surely do the trick." She leaned in close, and I willed my hands not to shake as I took the paper bag from her hands. "There's peach pie in there. But only if you eat your vegetables, right? You're still a growing boy." And with that obvious joke at my expense, given my six foot three frame and shoulders as wide as you'd think they would be, River McNee dissolved into peals of the most musical laughter I had ever heard.

"Hilarious, River." I tried to look miffed, but it was hard to feign hurt feelings when she was gifting me with that smile. "Since it's Friday, I would like to put my order in for next week," I said, grabbing the money out of my billfold to pay for the next week's lunches, the same as I did every Friday. It saved us all time that way, paying for the week ahead of time.

"You know, not that I want to turn down the money that earns me a living, but you'd save a lot if you packed your own lunches, you know?" River folded the bills without counting them and slipped them into the brown leather satchel she wore over one shoulder.

"I can't cook worth a damn, and even if I could, I wouldn't. If I packed my own lunches, I wouldn't get to see your sweet smile every day, River, and you can't put a price on that." I don't know where those accidentally smooth words came from, but I was both proud of myself and terrified at the same time. It was a blatant come on, and who knew how she would respond? I always got a few kind words from River when she brought lunches. She was always so pleasant and kind to everyone, but every time I tried to get more than a few sentences out of her, she rushed away like her skirt was on fire.

But she didn't move from her spot.

She froze, eyes downcast, looking at some mark I couldn't see, but seemed like it occupied one hundred percent of her attention. I wondered if she'd even heard me, until I saw the blush staining her cheeks. A flush of scarlet on her tanned skinned ran down her neck and disappeared under the neckline of that straining blue fabric.

How far down does that blush go? I was dying to find out.

I knew one thing—not only had she heard me, but she thought enough about my words to become flustered.

Pressing on, I pushed my luck a little further. "River, it's Friday. What are you doing this weekend?"

Surprised, she looked away from whatever interesting thing she had found on the ground and replied without thinking. "Helping the sisters with the washing, and then I don't know what else. I'm busy during the week; I plan little else on those days."

"So would you say you have free time?" I said, leaning my elbow on the side cart and wincing at the creaking noise as it gave a little under my considerable weight. I straightened immediately. The scarlet blood had not faded from her cheeks, and she was looking everywhere but at my face as she stammered out a reply.

She was embarrassed? This was fun. It was one thing if she wouldn't give me the time of day, but I was getting all kinds of fun reactions out of Miss River McNee today. She took a deep breath and met my eyes again. I dragged them up from her dancing button at just the right second so she didn't see me staring at her chest again. There's teasing a lady and then there's being a right ass. I wouldn't mind the first, but refused to be the second.

"Well, I don't really have much planned besides chores," she hemmed. Her eyes darted nervously over my shoulder and then back to me. She backed away from me and made as if to get back on her motorcycle. I didn't know what had her so spooked, but I wasn't letting her get away from me until I said what I had to say.

"It was nice to see you, Jonas." River tried to beat a hasty exit, but I grabbed her hand as she tried to slip away. It was strange how she kept looking around me, but not at me. Everything was fine until I asked her about the weekend. When I grabbed her hand, she froze, eyes wide and fearful, and her full pink lips parted in a little *o* shape.

"Woman, would you stop running?" My voice was louder than I meant it to be, but damn if I didn't need her to pay attention. I'd been trying for a month to ask her on a proper date, and this was as close as I'd come in that time. "You've been avoiding me for several weeks now, and I'd like more of a conversation than the time it takes for a good afternoon and exchange of a few coins."

Now I was a big guy, and I could intimidate without trying. With that in mind, I had been prepared for a few different reactions. There could have been outright refusal; after all, she was such a gentle lady, and I was a pretty clumsy oaf on my best day. I wasn't as smooth or handsome as Ian. I didn't have women fawning all over me all the time, so it took courage to even get the words out to River.

She could have laughed, thinking it was a joke. I knew women could react that way, as well. She could have reacted a dozen different ways, but I wasn't prepared for the sting in my arm as she pinched me as hard as she could, and with a scowl that completely changed the features of her face, hissed, "What is wrong with you, Jonas? Are you trying to get me killed?"

Say what now? She wasn't waiting for me to answer her question; she plowed right ahead, pulling one long braid over her shoulder in frustration.

"Do you not know where we are and *must you shout?*"

I still wasn't following, but she was mad enough to spit nails, so I tried to come up with an answer that would make her not be mad at me anymore.

"This is the only time I see you, River. I'd like to see more of you, but the only way to do that is to ask you, right? Did I do it wrong? Are you that opposed to spending time with me?" She must not have realized that I was still holding her hand as she had made no move to yank it back, so I released her and stepped back. "I can respect if you don't want to, but I'm not sorry I asked. If you want an apology because I kissed you in front of Callie's Trinkets, I didn't mean to embarrass you. But I won't say I'm sorry for being interested. We were on a date, River. First you acted like you wanted to be seen with me, and everything was going fine, and the next thing I know, you are pulling away and treating me like a regular customer. I won't understand if you don't tell me. Are you not interested in me anymore? Are you interested in someone else?"

Was she dating someone else now? Unthinkable. The thought of it made me sick, and I had to rein in the anger to keep my arms from turning to granite right in front of her. River's face was beet red now, and she raised her eyes to the sky and mumbled words that sounded suspiciously like a prayer for patience before she bit her lip and sighed.

"The first rule of the Jonas Pederson fan club is that Jonas Pederson belongs to everyone and no one."

"Come again?"

With a deep sigh, River threw her hands in the air and closed the gap between us. She placed one small hand on my forearm, and I gasped at the heat. Was I craving her closeness so much that my body burned at the touch? I wouldn't doubt it. I'd been thinking of her since the day I met her.

"Turn around and see what I mean."

I turned my head to oblige her, but all I saw behind me was Ian and his row of followers. They were all staring at us, though, and a few of the women had disgruntled looks on their faces. One blond girl on the end of the row was clutching a basket in her hands until her knuckles were white, and she narrowed her eyes, glaring daggers in our direction.

"Is that woman angry with me? If looks could kill, I'd have a spade through my forehead right now."

"Oh she's irate for sure, but not at you." River sighed again. "Jonas, could it be that you *are* that oblivious? You don't see all those women looking at you?"

I turned my head again. Of course I could see them; any fool with eyes could see them. I didn't know why they would be mad at me, though. "Who are we talking about? Ian's ladies?"

"Ian's . . . what?" River paused, her doe-brown eyes as wide as saucers before she laughed, a full rich laugh that rang like church bells. The sound was so beautiful to my ears, I would make a complete ass out of myself as many times as she liked if I could just hear her laughter again. She laughed until tears collected in the corners of her eyes and she had to fill her lungs with air again, the movement causing that poor overworked button on her dress to pull the sides of the fabric near to tearing.

"Jonas," River tried to speak, but her laughter caused the words to come out in gasps. "Those aren't Ian's women. That is a throng of hopeful ladies wishing you would turn your face to them. They come every day to get a glimpse of you. Look at them, all dressed up like it's Sunday, and you not even sparing a glance." River clutched her sides and bent over, her full laughter dying down to hysterical giggles. "You are prime bachelor real estate, Jonas, and you just broke no less than ten or twelve hearts by asking me on a date right here in front of them. I know if I lived in town, every one of their mamas would try to snuff me out in my sleep."

What? I turned to look again, and this time Ian was laughing, and the blond girl who was staring angrily now had tears in her eyes. When she saw me looking, she pivoted and with her back to me, walked away from the grassy lunch area. Within a second or two, the others followed, leaving only Ian standing off to the side, a stupid grin on his face and his cheeks puffed out with whatever food he'd swiped.

I still didn't understand, but the shrill whistle blow that filled the air around the yard told me one thing—lunch was over, and with it, my time with River. I hadn't even gotten an answer to my question yet, and I wasn't about to leave without getting it—even if she was trying to pack her cart and go while I turned my back. I flustered her, that much I knew, and until she gave me a solid no, I would take it as a maybe.

"Oh no, you don't." I put my hand on the side cart of the little motorbike, pinning it down as River swung her skirted leg over the seat and tried to start the bike. She couldn't figure out why it wouldn't go. Little did she know it was just a tiny bit of my strength that had that cart pinned in place.

"Oh, I don't what? You've wasted your whole lunch time chatting with me, and now you don't even have time to eat. Don't you need to get back to work?" River gave up trying to start the bike and crossed her arms over her ample chest with a huff. She looked angry, but the corners of her mouth quirked up regardless, and I saw it.

"They'll get their sweat off my back later for sure," I replied, confidence making my smile wide and lazy. The cart creaked under the light pressure of my hand, but it was going nowhere. "I can eat later, after I've gotten an answer to the question I've yet to ask properly. Miss River McNee, would you do the honor of being my date this Saturday afternoon and possibly into the evening a bit as well?" Were her eyes always this dark? So deep brown they appeared to be black, and the pupils two dark pools so wide they almost touched the whites. She mumbled something under her breath, and I paused. "Is that a yes or a no?"

Taking a deep breath, she squared her shoulders. "Will you protect me from the likes of Ginny Mickelson and the other girls who've hearts you squashed just now when they try to tear me limb from limb?"

The words mocked, but her eyes were serious. It seemed like a joke, but she needed reassurance, so I would give it to her.

"River, I'll not let anything happen to you when you're with me. Never. My body is your shield." It might have been a little overkill, but when had I ever been anything less than direct? Besides, this was the first time I'd got this far with River since she had become skittish on our last date, and I needed to use every opening I could get. I picked her hand up in mine and brought it to my lips for a quick, chaste kiss, once again marveling at the heat of her skin when we touched. It was a good sign, surely.

Sighing again, she pulled her hand from my grasp, and this time couldn't hide the smile from my eyes. "All right, but you'd better make it worth my while. I don't think you know what you've done today, Jonas Pederson, but you'll find out soon enough, I suppose. I'd be happy to spend Saturday afternoon with you, and some of the evening as well. Pick me up at four and be prepared to deal with the sisters when you do."

I felt Ian walk up behind me more than I heard him as I took my hand off the cart and River finally got the engine to turn over. I grinned and waved at her as she drove away, back out of town to the small home she shared with the Sisters McNee. My mood considerably lifted, my body feeling lightened after my conversation with River. I could move mountains today, if I wanted.

"Can you come back to work now, before we all get our hides chewed, loverboy?"

I laughed and slapped Ian on the shoulder, laughing even harder as he stumbled heavily under my light shove.

"I'll work circles around everyone else, and they know it. Let someone say otherwise." I wouldn't get into trouble for being late back from lunch, but I quickened my pace, just in case. "Can I ask you something, though? Aren't all those women always lined up to see you at lunch time? River made it sound like I destroyed some sacred lady trust when I asked her out on a date, but that can't be right."

Ian looked as if he'd swallowed a peach pit, his face screwed up so tight, and then he burst into laughter at my innocent question.

"Sometimes I like you, Jonas, and sometimes I want to knock you upside your giant skull. I'm so jealous of you, you thick son of a bitch." Ian turned to walk the short distance back to work but then paused, sniffed the air, then walked back and sniffed the space close to me. He looked around, didn't find what he was looking for, and threw his hands in the air before asking, "Why do you smell like smoke?"

CHAPTER 5

RIVER

I'd made it out of town and was mostly down the rough dirt road that led to the house I shared with the sisters before I realized I'd melted the grips on the handlebars of my bike. The acrid smell of burning rubber and foam reached my nose seconds before I saw the tiny tendrils of smoke wafting in front of my eyes. *Dammit.* What was it about Jonas Pederson that made me lose control?

I hated my fire and everything that had ever come from it, but just thinking about that giant of a man had me unable to stop the heat from rising to my skin. I may have hated my fire, but I did not hate Jonas Pederson.

And he had asked me for a second date.

In front of his entourage.

It was laughable, that he had plucked the words right out of a dream and told me he wanted to spend time with me, only me. What a pity he had to do it in front of half of the women in town of marriageable age. Women who'd had their eyes fixed on him for a while. Of all the rotten luck.

And he was right. I had been giving him the cold shoulder for the last few weeks. But it wasn't because he tried to kiss me in front of Callie's when we were walking through town. Rather, it was because I almost lit his hair on fire, I was so worked up over him paying attention to me. Remembering how I had barely caught myself in time sent shudders through my whole body. Sometimes I really hated myself. My hormones were a lit match looking for something to burn.

I pulled the motorbike into the side yard of the small white two-story house I shared with Alice and Meri. The house we'd inhabited for the last sixteen years—ever since the sisters had gotten frustrated with the Court and moved us out of the town proper. That was a long time ago, but the sisters were holding an uncharacteristically long grudge. I was free to do what I wanted to do, but Alice and Meri wouldn't move back inside Havenwood Falls until "that Bishop boy knocks on the door and begs." But we all knew that would not happen. No matter which Bishop "boy" was in question, we would never see a single one of those tall, dark, and handsomes banging on our door and begging forgiveness. The sisters didn't care. They felt I had been wrongfully evaluated as a child, and no matter how I felt about the subject, they would never be assuaged.

I opened the front door and tossed my apron and money satchel over the coat rack by the door. I didn't count the money, and I didn't worry about someone taking it. We lived comfortably enough out here in the woods, and no stranger was likely to come waltzing through our front door with nefarious intentions. The sisters' natural glamour made sure of that. People only found our home if the sisters willed it; otherwise, they could search forever and only find trees, tall grass, and wildlife. It was laughable really, considering I could see the Havenwood Falls sign next to the road from my front yard. It was the sisters' way of thumbing their noses at the Court of the Sun and the Moon all those years ago. I knew that as long as we weren't causing trouble, the Court wouldn't spare us a thought, and moving out of town didn't make them feel one way or another, but the sisters felt differently.

I didn't have the same aggravation or negative feelings. I loved Havenwood Falls, and I loved the sisters. They had blessed my life for the best from the moment I met the Sisters McNee—everything that had happened since then had been gravy.

Until Jonas Pederson, that is.

"River, what's the matter?" I passed through the house at top speed and out through the rear kitchen door to find Meri in the front part of the garden, a wide-brimmed hat pulled low over her eyes and her steel gray braid trailing down behind it. "You're all in a tizz. What's got you so worked up you're throwing sparks?"

"I'm not throwing sparks, Aunt Meri," I said, looking down at my hands just to make sure, considering I had ruined the handles of my bike. And who knew when I could get replacements? Motorcycles weren't common in these parts, and women riders even less so.

"Maybe not now," she said, straightening from the herbs she'd been stooping over and sliding her mini shears into her apron pocket. "But I smelled smoke on the wind, River—and Alice had a dream . . ."

Alice's dreams were nothing to laugh at, even if they were a little vague. After all, I also was once a dream Alice had.

"Oh." I stood next to Meri—we were the same height now—and took the basket full of herbs out of her arms as we both headed back through the kitchen door. "And what kind of dream would that be?"

We didn't quite make it all the way through the door before I heard a voice, huffing and puffing with exertion behind me. "We'll be getting a visitor tomorrow then, won't we? A handsome one, I'm thinking."

I didn't have to turn around to know Alice was smiling, but I did anyway. She was pushing a wheelbarrow filled to the brim with fruit—apples and pears, figs and peaches, all perfectly ripe for eating. The sisters used their Celtic nature magic to keep the small orchard at optimal conditions for growing at all times. Even in winter, we could tend the fruit trees. People had long since stopped trying to figure out how we could make our pies with fruit out of season, and we didn't volunteer the information. Of course she'd be out of breath from pushing that load. Handing Meri her basket through the kitchen door, I made my way back out into the yard.

"Barring your correct assumption, Aunt Alice, I told you to let me do these things. I'm stronger than I look, you know." I manned the wheelbarrow while she stood there chuckling, and Meri came back out the door with a couple of empty baskets. Among the three of us, we made quick work of emptying the wheelbarrow, sorting the fruit, bringing it all back into the large kitchen, and stacking it in the pantry shelves that were laid empty for just such a purpose.

"Care to tell me why such a large harvest today?" Normally we picked only what was needed for orders, and not so many different fruits at a time. Usually such a large harvest was for some catering function, like a wedding or a party, or for canning, but that wouldn't be until later in the fall.

"What kind of pie does Jonas Pederson like, River?" Meri asked, as she pulled the sugar and flour out of the cabinets and tied an apron around her waist.

"Yes, River, and I picked the figs and pears for you to take to Napoli's tomorrow. I'm guessing they will need them right about now, so please take them while you're out." Alice busied herself with pulling her rolling pins and dough cutter from the wooden drawers we kept them in and acted for all the world like there was nothing strange about her request.

"Did Napoli's place an order?"

"No, but I have a feeling."

"And what makes you think I know what kind of pie Jonas Pederson likes, hmm?" I murmured the question, but I already knew the answer, and it was just a farce even acting like it surprised me.

"I dreamed our young River would get a gentleman caller, and there is only one gentleman you would say yes to. You've only had eyes for him since you were just a teenager. Although the real mystery is why it would take so long for you two to get together. He's a man of thirty now, for goodness sake. And you are a woman in your own right."

"There are other ladies in town, you know," I admonished the older woman as I automatically washed the peaches that Meri pulled out of the pantry and handed to me. "Just because I've had a crush on him since creation doesn't mean he has any obligation to pick me out of the masses."

"But he did, River. He picked you. And he's coming tomorrow, and he's taking you to Napoli's or I'll bet double the money in that satchel by the door. Bet me." By the stubborn tilt to her chin, I knew I was better off not taking the bet. Besides, money didn't mean a whole lot to the sisters. They lived simply, and money was a means to get by, not something to be coveted. All extra funds went into savings I personally took to the bank in town. It had been like that since as long as I could remember, and probably since before then.

"You two are awfully well informed for rarely having been in town for sixteen years and not owning a telephone," I grumbled half-heartedly.

"We aren't hermits, River. We still get visitors, and we still talk to people." Meri cut a small x on the bottom of a peach and slid it into a pot of just boiling water.

"Yeah, we just get to be a lot choosier about the people we talk to." Alice hooted, her laughter catching on until all three of us were giggling in the kitchen like children. I knew the ladies moved out of town for me, but it made me happy to know the decision had not been such a burden to them. I would stay with them as long as they would have me—they were my family now.

And apparently, my family knew peach pie was Jonas Pederson's favorite.

CHAPTER 6

RIVER

*B*eing as young as I was and having such a limited view of the world, I didn't always have a keen grasp of my surroundings, but fear was a universal feeling. Everyone knew how to recognize that, and as I stared, wide-eyed, at the solemn faces of the people seated in front of me, I was cloaked in the inky black blanket of terror.

I was seven years old again—I hated this dream.

To the left of me, sitting at a table away from where I was placed, sat the sisters, who had saved my life and proclaimed themselves my protectors. They stared at the row of faces in front of us, their features tight and pinched, their eyes mirroring the same sternness.

"This isn't a hearing. It's a meeting." Meri slapped her hand on the polished wood table in front of her, silver curls bobbing against her ears. "So do you mind telling me then, why you're all lined up like ducklings?"

"Wrong metaphor, sister." Alice patted her sister's hand and clucked her tongue against her teeth. "Ducklings are sweet little creatures. The Court of the Sun and the Moon looks like it is ready to hand out a death sentence. I'll have you explain what's going on right now, if you would." Alice's voice was hard, a complete directional change from the soft even tone she had been using since I met her.

"You all knew we were bringing her home with us; we brought her here as a formality. You are treating her like a convict. She's a little girl, not a thief or a murderer."

My little legs shook with fear, and I put my hands in my lap to keep my knees from knocking together. Not a murderer. No, I wasn't, but I could have been. It wasn't lack of effort on my part that had kept me from ending that teacher at school. I hadn't been trying to kill him exactly, but I hadn't been thinking about *not* killing him either.

I'd only been with the sisters for a short time, essentially the time it took for us to travel from Carlisle, Pennsylvania, where they found me, to Havenwood Falls—all the way across the country and into the Colorado mountains. But in that short time, they'd shown me more kindness than I had found in the two years I'd been at the Carlisle school. They had not only saved my life, but they'd shown me that there were other people in the world like me. Maybe not exactly like me, but people with powers. They told me they would welcome me in Havenwood Falls.

But they met us with this.

"What is your name?" The tall, dark-haired man stood in front of me and spoke for the first time. Unlike the others in the room, he was the only one standing, and he regarded me with his unsmiling face, waiting for my answer. "Are you a mute? Your elder has asked you a question. What is your name? Surely you know it." His expression was as black as his slicked-back hair, and his eyes brooked no argument.

"River," I replied softly, not knowing what else to say.

"Is that all? No last name?" he prompted, looking both bored and irritated all at the same time. But I had no other information to give him.

"Rodavan, you're being obtuse," Meri admonished. I stole a nervous glance over my shoulder, and Alice winked at me. People yelled all the time. It couldn't be all bad if Alice was winking at me, could it?

"I'm just asking questions, Miss McNee. I don't intend to frighten, merely to learn all I can. With power comes responsibility, and it is the Court's responsibility to keep the residents of Havenwood Falls safe.

Especially considering our town's tragic . . . history." The man called Rodavan let his gaze drift around the room. A terribly intimidating man, he oozed authority. Dream me tried to recall the faces of everyone who sat across from me, but no matter how many times I tried, or how many times I had this same dream, I couldn't remember them. Even though I'd since seen them all many times over the last sixteen years, in this dream, when I was only seven again, everyone's face was a blur. Everyone but the Sisters McNee, Rodavan Bishop, and one other.

"What can you tell us, little girl? About yourself? About where you came from? Leave nothing out, because if you do, I'll know. I have no patience for liars." The voice behind Rodavan belonged to a striking man. So tall and slender, sitting straight up in his chair he was almost as tall as a normal man standing. Long silvery hair flowed just past his shoulders, and I would have thought it was the most interesting feature about him but for his eyes—so pale and frosty, they could freeze the breath in your lungs. And his voice. That wasn't the voice of a fragile man. He commanded just as much attention as Rodavan, if not more. I knew, when talking to this man, I dared not tell an untruth. Finding the small amount of courage afforded by Meri and Alice in the courtroom, I addressed the Court as bravely as I knew how.

"My name is River. At least that's what the translation is, I'm told. I've forgotten how my parents pronounced it, it's been so long. They died of a great sickness years ago. Long before the people from the government came and took the children from our native lands. They took us to a boarding school to teach us English and to leave behind our heathen ways. Kill the Indian, save the man." I said all these things without heat. I probably should have had hate in my heart for what had happened, but it was all I knew. And even now, it seemed a million years away. It wasn't happy or sad. It was just something that happened. It was my truth. "So when I tell you my name is River, I mean just that. I don't have the thing you refer to as a surname. If I did, I've long forgotten it. The people at the Carlisle school called me Mary Smith, but I don't recognize that name."

I focused on Rodavan when I was speaking, because even with his serious and stern face, it was still easier to look at him than at the older man behind him. There was something scary about him I couldn't place. Like he could see right into my mind.

"Something like that, River," the older man said, as if he could read my mind indeed.

"If you're done, Elsmed, may I continue my quest for answers?" Rodavan murmured, but not soft enough that the sisters didn't hear him.

"More like an inquisition," Alice grumbled. "I'd like to know what good comes from terrifying a child. You knew about me before we even left Havenwood Falls to get her. We sat in this very room while Meri told you my dream. You already know the circumstances, so why are we doing this right now?"

"Because you aren't the only one in this town who has premonitions." He didn't yell, but Elsmed's voice cut through the noise of the room regardless. "And Rodavan did some searching after you left. The results were . . . inconclusive."

"Inconclusive to you; I know what I saw." Rodavan was talking to Elsmed like I wasn't even in the room anymore, and what they were discussing was much more supernatural than just a girl who could spit fire from her mouth. I didn't know it at the time, being new to Havenwood Falls, but had learned since that Elsmed was fae, and Rodavan was a mage. One could read minds and the other could wreak havoc on them. They didn't just look scary—they *were*.

"Well then, stop beating around the bush and ask her what you want to know," Alice slapped her hand on the wooden desk again to show her displeasure. "Stop the bully session and let's get on with it. River, they want to know about your fire. That's all. Tell them what you told us."

With Alice's prodding, the words came out in a hurried rush. I spoke quickly, afraid that at any moment they would tear me away from the two women I thought of as my saviors. I told them everything. About my power. About how my parents taught me at an early age to hide it, to bury it and never use it, lest someone find out.

How they had died, and how it had terrified me when all the children were taken away. How I had lived at the school, trying to blend in, until the incident with Wesa—I choked up then, and the tears fell. Not only for Wesa, but for what had happened after I had used my fire on Mr. Crane. I'd done something bad, and they had almost put me to death for it. That's what they wanted to know, really. If I would do something like that again.

"I'm not a bad girl." I ended my story on a breathless sob. "I'm not bad. I don't want to hurt people. I won't use it again, I won't." It was my fire I referred to. And I wasn't making an empty promise. I wouldn't use it again. It scared the hell out of me. And what good was a power that hurt people anyway?

"She speaks the truth as she knows it," Elsmed said, not looking at me but at Rodavan, who needed the most convincing. There were feminine murmurs from the rest of the Court, but they were just white noise at this point. There may have been more conversation than what I remembered, but this was my dream, and as far as dreams went, it focused solely on what was important—Rodavan's words.

"She may speak *her* truth."

Rodavan turned to address the rest of the Court, turning so the only thing I could see was the back of his tailored waistcoat. "But trust me, I know what I saw. I can't see her future. All I see is flames. All-encompassing flames." He turned around and faced me again, his dark stare oddly enthralling, and even though I didn't want to look at him, I couldn't look away. "Someday, you will burn. The question is, can we afford to have you in Havenwood Falls when you combust?"

I AWOKE THEN, just like I always did at that part of the dream. I simply opened my eyes; I no longer woke up sweating or breathing heavily. I'd had the dream so many times, I could recite it in my sleep, so to speak. Rodavan had looked into my future and seen calamity. There was no arguing that. He was a powerful mage in his own right; if he saw it, it must be true. No one had argued with him after that, but neither had they come to a decision about what to do with me.

I smiled in my comfortable bed as I stared at the white-painted ceiling of my room, in the house that had been built just for Meri, Alice, and me. The sisters had interrupted the meeting in a flurry of anger and hurt feelings.

"We're not waiting around for you," they'd said almost in unison. "She's ours, and we don't need you to protect her. We can do it on our own."

And that was it. They moved out of Havenwood Falls as soon as they finished their new house. And it was finished quickly, because even though the people of Havenwood Falls didn't know me, a little native girl from halfway across the country, the Sisters McNee were beloved members of the community. No one wanted to see them go, but everyone for sure pitched in to make sure their new home was built quickly and comfortably.

This home. The one I lived in now, with Alice and Meri. The Court gifted us all with amulets that allowed us to come and go through town as we pleased. I didn't delude myself thinking they did it out of the goodness of their hearts. I knew it was because it helped them keep an eye on me. Even though we lived outside of town limits, we were still just barely within the wards, and those wards would ripple at the sign of trouble. Well, I'd been here for sixteen years with nary a burp in the wards, so I didn't have a care. Living *just* inside the wards was tricky, though. If we weren't careful, we would gradually lose our memory of the place, the more time and distance from the wards passed. That didn't stop the sisters from settling down outside the town limits, though. It may have seemed immature, but I think the sisters knew one day I would need Havenwood Falls, even if they didn't. Besides, for all their anger on my behalf, Havenwood Falls was their home, as well. And it was where all their friends lived.

The amulets allowed us all to stay close, and as someone who had been saved quite literally from the noose, I would take what I could get. And what I had was a loving home. I would never do anything to jeopardize that, no matter what Rodavan Bishop said. I no longer worried over anything he may have said when I was a child, considering both he and his brother had since been banished from

Havenwood Falls for using dark magic. My suppressed power was the least of anyone's worries these days.

~

I CHECKED the slim gold watch on my left wrist for probably the twentieth time in a matter of as many minutes. He was going to show up soon, and I still hadn't selected the right outfit. I picked at the pile of clothes on my bed in frustration. It wasn't that I had a lot to choose from, and I never paid much attention to the fashions in the first place, but . . .

My chest.

I had to admit it was a nightmare to choose a nice outfit because of my large chest. Both Alice and Meri told me to stop whining whenever I complained about my ample bosom, but they didn't have to pray for their buttons to hold, or press their forearms across their chests when running up and down the stairs to keep them from bouncing painfully. If I dared say anything, they would just tell me I shouldn't be running up and down the stairs.

The current fashion trends were shorter hemlines and loose cuts. Well, that didn't work for me because I was short of stature, so everything was long until Meri altered it for me. I couldn't sew a stitch. I could, however, get my motorcycle started in subzero winter mountain weather, so I tried not to let myself get too down about my lack of mending skills. And loose cuts? Sure, those worked if you were flat as an ironing board—which I was not.

I settled on a navy blue sleeveless cotton dress with a drop waist and a skirt that fell to just below my knees. I paired it with a peach cardigan that barely managed to stay buttoned if I left the top two undone. I rolled my shoulders after I put it on, just to test the strength of that third button, and it stretched at the hole a bit but held. I topped it off with a pair of nude Mary Janes and gave a twirl in the mirror. Perfectly presentable, if a little boring.

As much as I said I never cared much for fashions, I'd never been on a real date before Jonas, and the last one I went on was a disaster. It was a little embarrassing, but I just hadn't had an interest in any of the other young men in town. Not since I'd first laid eyes on Jonas Pederson when I'd started making regular deliveries six years ago. We'd never even spoken to each other until a year after that. I'd about given up hoping he would make a move other than to order lunch every day, especially with the throng of hopeful ladies all but throwing themselves at him every chance they had. Now not only had he asked me out once, but he was enamored enough he pursued me again, even after I tried so studiously to cut ties with him. After all that effort on his part, I wanted to look nice for him.

At the bottom of the stairs, I met Alice, who waited until I descended all the way before pressing something small and metallic into the palm of my hand. I should have known by the wicked gleam in her eye she was up to something. Turning my hand palm out, I found a shiny new penny.

"What's this for?"

Alice smiled with delight. "It's a good luck charm, River. Special magic for you if you're going to be seeing Jonas on a regular basis."

"Magic?" I'd seen the sisters do some amazing things, but a penny? That was new to me.

"Yes. You simply take the penny and place it between your knees when you're out with a handsome man . . ."

"Then what?" I still didn't understand.

"Nothing—you leave it there. As long as that penny is held up by your knees, there is no way for a handsome devil to make his way between them."

And then she opened her mouth and laughed. Side-splitting laughter spilled from her while I stood on the bottom step, holding a penny in my hand, and realizing that I, River McNee, a girl who had almost lit up like a candle the man who'd given her her first kiss, had just been the butt of a sex joke told by an old lady. Red-faced and shaken, I didn't even have time to think of a suitable response before the knock on the door commanded all of our attention.

CHAPTER 7

JONAS

J'd been given my second chance. I'd braved the sisters, left with my dignity intact, and gotten some precious alone time with River, only to come across another obstacle as soon as we were seated at Napoli's Ristorante Italiano. An obstacle sitting so close behind me, I could feel him staring through the back of my head.

Gabriel Doyle. *Yay.*

I don't know how I missed him when we walked in, but somewhere between the charcuterie board and the Tuscan rabbit stew, I glimpsed him, slightly to the left and behind me at a private table in a dimly lit corner. Watching us.

Not that I didn't care much for Gabriel. He'd helped me out a time or two, and I maybe owed him a few favors, but he took a special interest in River McNee. Now we were occupying the same space at the same time, and there was no way he would leave us alone. That was my fault.

I'd gone to him for help, a little information, against my better judgment after River dropped me like a hot rock. Everyone who's anyone knew better than to get under Gabriel Doyle's thumb, but I was confused and desperate at the time. And no one knew how to get unobtainable information better than Gabriel and the Lilith Nest, unless you counted Roman Bishop, and I wasn't about to ask that guy for a hand crawling out of hell. There were jackasses, and there were *irredeemable* jackasses.

Gabriel Doyle was just the regular kind.

I hadn't known River's history with the Court when she came to Havenwood Falls, but after meeting with Gabriel, I knew a lot more. Things I shouldn't know unless she told me. Things she would be upset to know I found out from Gabriel Doyle, dammit. All I wanted to do was court my lady, but the back of my neck was crawling with the stare of a bored rich vampire with lots of power and a need to meddle in the affairs of others. There was no way he would leave us alone.

I was right.

Even if I couldn't feel him approach, I could see the fear in River's eyes as he walked up and stopped directly in front of our little table off to the side of the kitchen. Her gaze had gone from friendly to apprehensive to downright terrified as she took in his perfectly tailored suit, his dark slicked-back hair, and sardonically raised brow. It wasn't the way he was dressed that scared her. It was probably the fact he was a vampire, and a powerful one at that. He was also insufferably handsome, and I didn't want him anywhere near my River.

Go away, Gabriel! I hissed in my mind. His mouth quirked at the corner as if he could hear the thoughts running through my mind. That ass knew he was intruding, and he for certain did not care.

"It's rare I see you in town outside of your business hours, Miss McNee," he said smoothly, bending slightly at the waist as a courtesy. River was not impressed, and she tried to keep her face free from expression, but I witnessed the tightening around her eyes.

"I might not live within the town limits, Mr. Doyle," she said, "but I'm sure you're well aware I have leave to come and go as I please."

"Can we help you with something, Gabriel?" I cut in. I didn't know why he was pressing River, but I wouldn't let him harass her, especially in front of me. Gabriel smiled a predatory smile that made his cold blue eyes turn up at the corners. That idiot was having fun.

"I was simply saying hello. I haven't seen River much in the last few years and wanted to inquire about the sisters. Are they in good health? You know we would love for them to come back and live in town again."

"The sisters are fine, but I'll extend your regards. Although I find your concern about them strange. Why do you care?"

I knew River's history and how it pertained to the sisters, having been informed by Gabriel previously, but I wisely kept it from showing on my face. Gabriel was silent for a moment, almost pensive even.

"River, you weren't banned from living in Havenwood Falls, from what I understand," he said, his voice low, so as not to attract attention from other diners.

"No, but I wasn't welcomed either. You weren't there, Gabriel, but you act awfully well informed. The Court thought to label me as a threat."

"But they didn't."

"Only because the sisters decided for everyone. They uprooted their home and left it all behind to start new. For me." The atmosphere was frigid as River ground out the words from between clenched teeth. "They made that decision to protect me, no one else. So please don't make it sound like you have some interest in the affairs of the sisters or me. You are not a member of the Court. Nothing we do should matter to you whatsoever."

Gabriel looked amused by River's candor, but my chest swelled with pride at the steel in her spine. He may have been giving her a hard time, but she damn well was dishing it right back. I didn't think I had ever been more attracted to her than I was in that moment, her gaze fierce and unyielding, her chest heaving with emotion. My eyes flickered down a bit at the thought of the heaving, noticing the button, or as I fondly referred to it, "my button," was pulling at the threads of the fastening on her sweater. Averting my gaze so I wouldn't get in trouble for looking overly long at something I shouldn't, I found I wasn't the only one who found that button fascinating.

Anger, hot and quick, shot like a rifle through my blood, and the change happened so fast, I couldn't stop the thickening of my blood or the roughness of the voice that resembled stone grating against stone as I barked out one quick word.

"Gabriel." *You will not look at her.* I left the second part unsaid, but I infused every part of his name with my intent. *No. Mine. Avert your eyes.*

It was River's startled face that had me regaining my control. I absolutely could not, would not, let my other self burst forth inside Napoli's. Not if I wanted to keep the sheriff from jumping up my ass. Not if I wanted to stay in Havenwood Falls. More importantly, it wasn't the side of me I wanted to show River either.

"I apologize," Gabriel said, and he *almost* looked like he meant it. "I did not intend to foster any hostility; I merely wanted to extend my regards. I'll leave you to yourselves, but please accept my apologies again. I hope to see you around more often, River. I must say, when Jonas came to me *begging* for information about you, the strength of his feelings impressed me."

Always one to get the last word in—that was Gabriel. While River stared at me, open-mouthed at the bomb Gabriel had just dropped, he walked away from the table, straightening his jacket as he went, looking for all the world like he'd gotten exactly what he wanted.

"Don't give me that look, woman." I grabbed hold of the situation right out of the gate while her mouth opened and closed like a fish on dry land. "I told you I went a little crazy when you started avoiding me. I had my reasons, and they were honorable . . . as far as reasons go."

River clapped her mouth shut with a snap. "I wouldn't say going to Gabriel Doyle for information was crazy." She sighed irritably. "I would say it shows questionable judgment, but you aren't crazy." She was embarrassed; the pink tinge of her cheeks told me so.

"Look, River, Gabriel isn't a bad guy; he's just a bit of an ass is all. I've had other dealings with him in the past. He's done me a few favors, to be honest." I didn't tell her that those favors came at a steep price. There were some things a gentle lady didn't need to know. I'd said Gabriel wasn't a bad guy. And he wasn't, at least not to me. He wasn't necessarily a good guy either.

"Gabriel Doyle does what is good for Gabriel Doyle. It so happens, thus far, that it has all been parallel to what you consider acceptable.

But I was quite enjoying our evening and our delicious dinner. I don't want to wreck it with more talk about that vampire. But I have to ask —and because it's painful for me, I ask you to be gentle in your judgments of me—what did he tell you?"

Because she was wringing her hands in agitation and for no other reason than I sought to comfort her, I took both of her small delicate fingers in mine. "You'll get no judgments from me, River McNee. I'll tell you everything I know, and if there is an untruth there, you can tell me. I simply wanted to know more about you, and was desperate to find a reason why you pushed me away. There was no other cause for my actions at all, but if I've hurt you by doing so, I'm sorry. I'm serious about you, and I thought we were making a connection. So when you cut me off, I was confused. I just wanted to know why."

It was the truth, and she could take it or leave it, but my heart was thumping in my chest so loudly, I was sure she could hear it. She wasn't looking at me, though, but at the way I held her hands in mine. She made no move to pull away, so I took it as a positive sign.

"Did he tell you what I did? What I am? I wonder how he knows." She whispered the words into the checkered tablecloth.

"You mean, did he tell me how you almost died when you were younger? About that horrible school and the mistreatment you withstood? Yes, he did. Or at least what he learned from his vast network connections." I didn't ask him how he got the information he did. I probably wouldn't like the answer.

"Did he give you that information for free?"

"Nothing is free, River, but he didn't ask for anything I wouldn't have given anyway." Gabriel Doyle never did something for nothing, but it wasn't anything she needed to worry about. "If you're thinking he fed from me, then I can tell you that didn't happen either. I don't make good vampire food." Not that I didn't taste good to vampires; it was that they literally couldn't feed from me. I was a Scandinavian stone man, and no matter how hard they tried, a vampire could not get blood from a stone. It was funny to watch them try, though.

River lifted her head and looked at me then, really looked at me, and maybe it was the candlelight, but her eyes looked blacker than their normal deep brown. She spoke, her lips quivering just slightly as she said, "Are you afraid of me too?"

It floored me. Was I afraid of her? What in the actual hell kind of question was that?

"The only thing I'm afraid of, River, is you telling me you don't feel the same things I do, and that you don't want to see me again. As far as your personality or the things you're capable of, I'll make my own character judgments, thank you. I'm enough of a man to tell my own mind. But just because you seem so worried about it, I'll tell you this—I'm not putting stock in a vision someone had more than sixteen years ago. There's truth in everything, but there is also room for interpretation. It doesn't look like anyone bothered to look too deeply into what Rodavan Bishop or Elsmed Fairchild saw when they tried to look into your future. They didn't see me there, did they? That can't be right, because I plan on being a large part of all of your tomorrows if you'll let me."

Please don't ask how I know all this right now, I pleaded silently. While most of us in Havenwood Falls with supernatural backgrounds generally knew of each other, we didn't run around proclaiming our sordid histories to each other, and unless a person could sense it on their own, we didn't go around announcing our magical heritage either. I'd never run around town yelling "I can shape-shift into a giant rock man," so River wouldn't know that about me. By rights, I shouldn't know a damn thing about her dealings, or her power.

But I couldn't plead my case, not after what I'd just said. That was about as smooth a line as ever had come out of my mouth, and I couldn't think of another word to say after that. It didn't matter, because I felt the squeeze of her fingers in mine, and I knew even if she said nothing in return, she heard me. She heard me just fine.

"I hate my power, Jonas." This time I wasn't imagining the sheen in her eyes, the tears that collected in the corners and threatened to fall. "And just so you know, I didn't push you away because I didn't want to see you again. My feelings for you . . . I . . ." She faltered on the words. "I can't control myself around you, Jonas. My body gets hot when you're close, and my insides go all a mess. The pressure builds up to where I think I will explode with it, and I don't know about you, but me and the word explosion aren't a good omen. While I want to be with you all the time, I think . . . I think I might be allergic to you? Or something like that. I've spent my whole life suppressing those flames and for me to not be able to control them around you— Well, I never want to hurt you. I don't want to hurt anyone, never again, but I wouldn't be able to live with myself if I hurt you."

I sat there dumbfounded while she told me that my nearness caused her to lose control over her body, and I tried very hard not to lose control of my own. Lustful thoughts be damned but she was serious. She thought there was something wrong with her. How innocent was River? I knew the sisters had raised her, but surely she knew something of what went on between a woman and a man? Allergies weren't her problem. Dealing with her desire was.

But I couldn't tell her that. At least, not right this moment. I could only continue holding her warm hands in mine and try to think of something to say to make her feel better.

"You can't be allergic to me, River. It's not possible," I said as I thought about my people and our predisposition to becoming men made of solid rock. "I'm a stone man. I'll not make you sneeze."

I don't know if she thought I was crazy or lying or both, but I was still grateful for the laughter that burst from her throat, and the tears that ran down her cheeks were of mirth, of that much I was certain. She kept laughing while I paid the bill and was still chuckling to herself as I held her sweater over my arm and walked out of the restaurant with her. The night air was warm, at least for those of us used to the mountain summer nights, and the street was deserted. I was feeling good about the evening until we rounded the side of the strip of buildings and took a turn around the back. The lighting was poor on this end of the street, and River stumbled over a loose sidewalk slate.

Fearing she would turn her ankle, I caught her as she fell and propped her up against the bricks behind her, focusing only on keeping her from injury.

I swear to the gods that's what I was thinking.

Until I stumbled myself, and instead of catching my body with the brick wall next to me, I found myself pressed chest to chest with one incredibly soft River McNee, her arms reaching around my back to keep me from knocking her to the ground.

There wasn't self-control on this earth to keep the groan from leaving my body.

I should have released her. I should have. But there was something about the warmth of her soft curves against the hard—and getting harder—planes of my own body that held me immobile. I couldn't let her go. Instead, I threw caution to the wind and buried my head in the crook of her neck, inhaling the scent that was uniquely River. Leaves on the wind, a campfire on a fall day, bliss. I felt her hands tighten against my back, an almost imperceptible grasping of her fingers into my flesh through the layer of my cotton shirt.

"River." I groaned again at the effort my words were costing me. "I want to kiss you right now."

"We shouldn't," she whispered, and I felt the skin of her throat move against my lips as I nuzzled my face even deeper into her hair. She shivered, and the vibration ran through my entire body. I could not move away on my own.

"I'll need you to be more firm, then, because I don't know that I'm strong enough to let you go at the moment. After all, anyone can see us." I didn't give a damn if the whole town was watching.

"There's no one here at all," she mused, her lips curving up into a smile. She wasn't helping matters at all, not with her feet lifting up on her toes so she could press even closer to me, the heat of our bodies becoming a tangible force.

"River, that isn't a no." And this time I couldn't stop myself from tasting her, from laying my lips against the skin of her neck then upwards across her chin. Just little nibbles. Not too much. Surely she would push me away any moment, and I would have to apologize. Beg forgiveness for the liberties I was currently taking.

But she didn't push.

She pulled.

Pulled me in just a little bit closer as she rose on her tiptoes, and as

I raised my head again, it was her hot mouth that captured mine. And even if it was my tongue that swept inside her mouth, she opened it all of her own volition. River McNee wanted me, and her desire was scorching hot. Gods help me, I wanted it to burn me up.

One hand crept up to her breast and squeezed, filling with the flesh I had only dreamed about for the last however long. Probably as long as I'd known her, who knew? She moaned into my mouth and wriggled against me, trying to push herself more fully into my grasp. We were both gone, so lost in each other that neither of us heard the spark or smelled the smoke. Neither of us noticed the flames until they traveled from River's arms and arced between us. I felt the heat through my shirt and down to my skin, and it was only then I smelled the acrid scent of burning cloth.

My shirt was on fire. With a startled shriek that pierced the silence of the night, she pushed me away and stood there, horrified as the flames licked her skin, sputtered and went out. As quickly as they had appeared, they were extinguished, and so was our moment. My body mourned the warmth of hers, but she wasn't the only one who'd had an unwanted reaction. One look at my right arm had me swiftly hiding it behind my back lest she see how my body had reacted to the flames.

While she stared at the ground, unable to meet my eyes, I flexed my fingers into a fist, out of sight, and willed my arm to return to normal. I willed the stone to become blood and bone again, to recede from the granite gray to the normal tones of the flesh. I wasn't ready for River to see that side of me yet, and she was already worked up as it was.

"I hurt you. I hurt you. I'm so sorry, Jonas. I swore I'd never . . . and I did. I didn't mean to, but it happened regardless. I don't . . . I can't . . ." She hadn't hurt me, not really. My body naturally reacted to preserve itself, so her flames did nothing more than scorch my shirt— but there would be no telling her that now. She was working herself up into a frenzy of guilt.

"River," I said, trying to choose my words carefully to keep her calm. "It's fine. I'm not hurt—look." And I waved my now normal arms in front of her, thankful that I had stopped the change in time.

"Jonas, you don't understand. I caught you on fire just because you kissed me. I lost myself. I had no control. Can you imagine if something more were to happen between us? You don't understand—this is exactly what Rodavan meant when he saw my future. Flames. Chaos. Destruction. If we continue to see each other, I'll burn you up. I never want do that to you. I'd rather never see you again than hurt you."

I opened my mouth to argue, but the tears running down her cheeks were enough to close it again. She was distraught. Anything I had to say to her then would fall on deaf ears.

"Jonas, please take me home."

And I did. The ride out of town was silent, marked only by the rattling of my Model T truck, the one I had serviced recently but still sounded like it would blow apart at any minute. She didn't say a word as she left the vehicle and went into the white house with the darkened windows. It didn't look like anyone was waiting up for her, but then again, I wouldn't put anything past the Sisters McNee. It was up to River what story she would tell them, but I knew one thing—there had to be a way to fix this thing with River.

It seemed her flames were attached to her emotions. The stronger the emotions she was feeling, the more out of control the flames. I smiled to myself as I maneuvered the truck back onto the road and started the long drive back to town. She was forgetting one thing. Yeah, she had a problem all right, but this was Havenwood Falls. We were all a little different, a little strange. There were many supernatural issues and ways to solve them. If she thought avoiding me was her best option, then River McNee had another think coming.

She wasn't doing this alone. Not anymore. Never again. I'd sell my soul to the devil if it meant keeping River.

CHAPTER 8

RIVER

*U*nbelievable. Not only was no one waiting up for me when Jonas dropped me off at home, for which I should have been grateful, neither of the aunts asked me for any details of the evening when we all got up for breakfast the next morning.

"Can't talk now, the pears are ready for picking today," Meri had cheerfully called as she'd walked out of the kitchen with no other explanation. Alice said nothing, just looked at me sadly and followed her sister out the back door, leaving me to wonder just how much those banshee sisters knew and the extent of their powers. Regardless, they left me alone, with no words of wisdom to lift the cloud of gloom over my head.

And then Monday came, and Jonas wasn't at the mine for lunch either. Not that I wanted to see him. Actually, it was the opposite—I wanted to avoid running into him, but still. It struck me in the heart to not see him lining up like the rest of the men to pick up lunch. I was out of sorts for sure, but I knew I made the right choice. I wish I felt better about it, especially since I could still taste Jonas Pederson on my lips every time I had the misfortune of thinking about it. Which was too often.

"Um . . . River? Can I have my lunch now?"

Two blinks. That's what it took to tear my thoughts away from a certain blond-haired blue-eyed giant who seemed to occupy the air I breathed even when he wasn't around. I came here every day with lunch orders for busy mine workers who either didn't have a knack for cooking to pack their lunches, or those that could but just had a taste for having me do it for them. It was easy money for me. Every day, I packed the orders from the day before and included a thick slice of whatever delicious confection Alice and Meri had ready, filled the side cart of my motorbike, and set off into town. I brought home orders and restaurant orders as well—but hitting the mine at noon bell was by far the most lucrative for me. And right now in front of me, one such hungry miner was standing, hand out in expectation.

"I am so sorry, Ian," I exclaimed, grabbing the brown paper sack with his name on it and handing it off with a sloppy grin. "I'm so distracted today. I don't know what came over me." I slipped the coins from his hand into the leather satchel I kept slung around my shoulder, listening with satisfaction as they clinked against the pile of coins already gathering at the bottom.

"Not too distracted to take my money though, I see," Ian grumbled, his dark facial hair doing nothing to hide the grin playing along the corners of his mouth.

"Well, if I ever get that distracted, Ian, might as well put me in a hole in the ground."

I liked Ian. He was only a little older than me and a normal human. One of many that populated Havenwood Falls, but Ian was a little more aware of the rest of us than most of the people who lived in town. Funny thing was, he never made a stink about it. Ian had been to see the sisters before and took their "otherness" in stride. None of us were any different from anyone else to Ian. I wish I had the luxury of being so blissfully ignorant.

"If you're looking for Jonas, he's not here today. Something came up."

I could imagine that something was me, and his need to avoid me after I set him on fire just a few days prior, but I couldn't say that to Ian.

"I'm not looking for him. I don't know why you would think that," I murmured under my breath. I'd meant it to come out louder, but my lungs froze up on the lie.

"Yeah, okay, River," Ian mumbled, opening the brown bag and tearing the wax paper away before ripping off a bite of roast beef sandwich and chewing. "You two are so weird, you deserve each other. God, this is good." He continued to chew, leaning against the side of my cart without a care in the world. Or apparently a place to be, as he seemed in no hurry to leave me be. "I don't know your story, but that guy has it bad for you. And you run him ragged, making him chase your skirts day after day. You're a real nice girl, River, but if you can't be serious about Jonas, then you need to cut him loose. It isn't right."

Cut him loose? My chest squeezed at the thought. Even though the advice was solid, I deserved it, and it was what I was trying to do, it still hurt to hear it.

"What do you know about Jonas?" I asked Ian, wondering just how much he knew about the man who had just hinted at his otherness before, but never quite come out with the specifics until recently.

"I know enough to tell you that's something you should discuss with him, and not with me." Ian winked before shoving his face full of food again. "What do *you* know about him?"

Thinking back to our conversation from the night before, I spoke. Ian may have been friends with Jonas, but I didn't know how much he knew. Some things were private.

"Well, I know he doesn't have an animal." Doesn't *have* an animal was polite speech for he doesn't *turn into* an animal. You know, because some people did.

"Why do you think that?" Ian had swallowed his food and now regarded me thoughtfully.

"Because he said I couldn't be allergic to him, because he was hypoallergenic." I was only being half serious, but I still didn't expect the belly laugh that exploded out of Ian with a force great enough for him to drop his sandwich on the ground. The laughter cut off as he realized what he'd done, and staring mournfully at the food in the dirt, he sighed.

"River, that was your fault. You made me laugh, and look." He pointed sadly at the ground.

"Here, take this. It was Jonas's anyway."

He smiled as he took the extra bag lunch from me. "Thanks, River, you're an okay girl. Try not to be too hard on Jonas, all right? He's my friend, and a good man. He deserves better than the runaround."

I didn't have time to answer him because he had turned and walked away, across the grassy field, his hand already digging another sandwich out of the brown paper bag. It wouldn't have mattered if he'd stayed; I had no good answer to give him. Ian may have had knowledge of what was going on in this town, but that didn't mean he was equipped to handle my type of baggage.

Ian was it. He was the last in line, and no matter how I strained my eyes and neck looking, Jonas was gone. It was fine. It was better that way, but I would be a liar if I said it didn't hurt. A lot. That was probably the reason that, instead of turning around and going down the long winding road back home, I kept riding my motorcycle toward town. Maybe it was that melancholy ache in my chest, the wanting of things I couldn't have, that had me stopping outside of the elementary school.

There was nothing wrong with it as far as schools go, but since I didn't live in town, I didn't have the option to attend. I missed nothing growing up, because the sisters saw to my education well enough, and even took my reading, writing, and arithmetic skills above and beyond what a young woman like myself might have learned. If I hadn't been so adamant about not using my powers ever again, I might have ended up at the Academy, but there was no reason for me to go if I didn't need to learn. Besides, no one else knew what I was, anyway. Still, I parked my bike outside of the schoolyard and sat there for a little while, caught up in the wistful wonderings of what might have been had I been born a normal child. This was Havenwood Falls. If I'd been born a normal child, I'd never have even seen this place.

It must have been the same whim that sent me in the school's direction in the first place that caused me to notice the figures leaving the school yard. It was otherwise empty—there was no reason for anyone to be in the place at all, considering it was July, and the primary term ran from September to May. There were neither children nor teachers required to be on property, so what were those two figures doing, wearing formal clothing and walking away from the school as if they had business there?

It didn't concern me. I shouldn't have paid any attention, but there was something about the bowler hat the older man wore that prodded a memory I had kept buried for a long time. And even something about the younger man with him, something about the sun-burnished color of his skin, and his features, which even from far away seemed so similar to mine and so oddly out of place in this hidden town in the Colorado mountains. There were other native people here, but even from a distance, they looked so *familiar*. But how could they? I didn't know them.

But I did. And it wasn't until they came closer to the place where I stood, frozen next to my motorbike, that I realized why I shouldn't have come here. The mustached face. The bowler hat. The mustache had more gray in it than brown anymore, and his once large frame had shrunken considerably, but I knew the name that went with the face I now recognized.

Hank Weisman. The man that lamented my fate as he left me bound in a shed to await my punishment. And the younger man next to him, with skin like mine and the features of a people I'd almost forgotten my connection to, was Wesa. Now he was fully grown into a man with a thin jagged scar on his chin—but still Wesa.

They pulled up short when they reached the spot where I stood. Mr. Weisman reached a hand up to tip his hat in polite greeting, and I almost thought I could get away with a smile without being recognized, but I couldn't be that lucky. His hand froze on the brim of his hat, Wesa's brown eyes widened, and both men gasped their surprise.

"Mary? It isn't you. It can't be you."

Rooted to the spot, my breath froze in my lungs. This wasn't good. They shouldn't be here. They had no reason to be here.

"I'm sorry." I tried to be polite yet distant, all while throwing my leg over my bike seat and cursing myself for wearing such a long skirt that made maneuvering difficult. Trousers would be more practical. "I'm not who you think I am. My name isn't Mary."

"River," Wesa finally spoke. His voice, no longer that of an angry little boy, carried with it the deep timbre of a man. "River, it's you. There's no one in this world with hair like that, and you still wear it in the same braids you did when we were kids. Dark black with ribbons of red and orange flowing through it. It's you—but how? You died. They said you died."

I knew who "they" were. The Cranes. Those nasty evil people who tried to take my life from me.

"I'm sorry. I'm not her. Now, if you'll excuse me, I need to be going."

Keep calm, keep calm. The words ran on a loop in my mind. Nothing good would come from this, I was sure. These people shouldn't be here in Havenwood Falls. Thinking about how close they had come to the sisters made my skin clammy and my stomach heave. They had to have ridden right past my house to even get here. I swung my leg over the side of the bike and had almost got it started before I heard the sobbing behind me.

"It *is* you. Mary. I'm so happy . . . so happy to see you." Mr. Weisman crumpled a little, his shoulders shaking and his gnarled hands reaching for my own. Frozen with shock, I could only let him do it, feeling his bony fingers curl around mine and squeeze. "I've always regretted . . . I mourned you . . . I've regretted every day the part I played. To see you alive again, I'm so joyous, Mary." I didn't know where this breakdown came from, but it was obvious I would not bluff my way out of this one. And there was something so heartbreaking about watching an old man fall over himself to apologize. There was one thing to get straight before we continued with the conversation.

"My name isn't Mary. It never was. My name is River McNee."

IT TURNED out that the reason those two were in Havenwood Falls, and at the school no less, was because Wesa was a teacher and the two of them had traveled to Havenwood Falls in response to a "Colorado call for educators." Apparently, there was a shortage of people who wanted to shape young minds. Who knew?

I couldn't believe it. Little Wesa all grown up and teaching primary school. Shortly after I had "died," things had taken a turn for the dangerous at the Carlisle school. Government regulations were becoming stricter against teachers and their treatment of the native students. There was reform in the works, but even so, it would take more than a few regulations to make Carlisle an upstanding school. At least in my mind.

As we sat in the grass at the edge of the empty schoolyard, Mr. Weisman explained what had happened in the years since I'd been gone, with Wesa filling in the details when Mr. Weisman, whether from old age memory failure or just overwhelming emotion, couldn't continue. Wesa—Mr. Weisman still called him Thomas—explained that both Mr. and Mrs. Crane had met with terrible ends. Mrs. Crane had died in a kitchen accident, and Mr. Crane had shot himself in mourning.

Wesa's voice had gone flat when talking about the Cranes, but I could imagine there was no love lost there. Mr. Crane was the one who had beaten a young Wesa all those years ago, right in front of me. *That scar on his chin is probably from that incident,* I supposed. Thinking of the Cranes made my neck itch; I could still feel the rough fibers of the noose as they tightened it around my neck like a leash. Horrible people. I couldn't scrounge up even a flash of sympathy for them.

Wheezing and coughing interrupted my negative thoughts, and I looked at Mr. Weisman, startled, noticing not for the first time how ancient and worn out he looked. Nothing like the large imposing instructor he'd been when I was a child. *Time changes everything, I suppose.*

"We just stopped by to look at the school today," Wesa murmured as he patted Mr. Weisman on the back, rubbing his hand in soothing circles as the coughing subsided. "I have an interview in two days, and we were just taking a quick look. We weren't prepared to stay outside for long, and I think he might be adjusting poorly to the mountain air."

I didn't doubt he was having difficulty breathing. For people who had spent little time in the mountains, adapting to the thinner air could be difficult. And given his age, and considering a possible compromised immune system, it would be a lot for anyone to adjust to.

"You should probably let him take a rest, Wesa," I mentioned, still feeling oddly detached from both people who had been so closely connected to my past. "Where are you staying?"

Wesa looked over his shoulder in the direction of the town's square. "We're staying at Whisper Falls Inn at the moment. If the teaching position is offered to me, then we'll look for more permanent housing, but for now the inn it is."

I nodded; that made sense. There was no reason for me to stick around either, but Wesa's eyes were speaking to me without words, so I paused before saying goodbye.

"River, you keep calling me Wesa, but you should know I go by Thomas now. I have since I was young."

"I'm sorry. I didn't mean to offend you," I stammered, embarrassed because I assumed that like me, he didn't want to be called by the name that Carlisle had forced on him. I guess it didn't occur to me that after all he went through as a child, he would want to carry anything with him from that place, least of all his identifier.

"No, it's all right," he said as he helped Mr. Weisman to his feet. "I wanted you to know, especially if we will be staying in Havenwood Falls. I kept the name Thomas because it's more professional. People are more apt to hire a teacher named Thomas Weisman than they are a Cherokee man named Wesa."

I flinched inwardly. Living so long near Havenwood Falls had been both a blessing and a curse. I'd almost forgotten about how the rest of the world operated. We didn't have as much of that prejudice around here. After all, Havenwood Falls was where the *really* different folk gathered. Hopefully neither Wesa nor Mr. Weisman would ever find out just how different. It also didn't escape my notice that Wesa, or Thomas as he preferred, now carried Mr. Weisman's last name as well. Just what kind of relationship did they have? Had Mr. Weisman adopted him?

"River, I'd like to see you again, if I could." Thomas caught my attention again with that statement. He'd been glad to see me, sure, but the look in his eyes was like something I'd seen before in how Jonas had looked at me, and I wasn't sure how to respond to it. I recognized that male interest, but I couldn't return it. Not when my heart was still shattered over what I had almost done to Jonas. "There's just so much I want to know about how you came to be here. How have you lived? Who took care of you?"

I couldn't tell him any of those things, especially not the truth. Because no matter the history I had with Thomas and with Mr. Weisman, they could never know how I came to be here. That would require breaking all of the rules I had been bound by. I might not live inside the limits of Havenwood Falls, but the wards still protected me, and the sisters as well. I loved this town, and I didn't want to ruin any part of it by breaking the rules. I would have to tell them something, though. Thomas would need an answer, and I needed time to come up with something suitable.

"I've some time in the morning tomorrow." I hesitated on the words. I wasn't so sure I wanted to talk to the sisters about this yet. They would find out soon enough, but I didn't want them to worry if I told them someone from my Carlisle past had shown up in Havenwood Falls. They might feel compelled to interfere. I didn't want them to have the burden of that kind of worry. I could handle this, I was sure. "I have my deliveries to make in the afternoon, but I can spare some time to meet, if you'd like."

Wesa liked that idea. He offered to meet me at my home, but that was a little too personal for me. The thought of him meeting the sisters made me uncomfortable, so I offered to meet him in town instead. As I watched him help Mr. Weisman into a car and drive in the inn's direction, I could only marvel at how very different both men were from my memories. Was Mr. Weisman really just a doddering old man after all this time? And Thomas? Just what kind of man had he become?

CHAPTER 9

JONAS

*I*t wasn't that I hated owing Gabriel Doyle a favor, although that brought its own complications to the table. I just didn't know he would call it in so soon, and that it would require me to be away from the mine and, in that vein, away from River, just when I needed to be right in her face. Because that was the only way to handle her—catch her attention before she had time to get lost in her own head and overthink.

I had no intention of giving River her space. I had every intention of going to work and showing up last in her lunch line, showing her I would always be there, that she couldn't scare me away. Instead, I was spending the day playing the sidekick for Gabriel because he needed someone to deliver black-market goods. Not what I thought I'd be hauling with my truck when I built the custom covered wagon bed two years ago.

"Does it bother you I asked you to do something outside the law like this?" he asked me after I finished the last run and stopped at his office to confirm the details and deliver the money I'd collected. The question surprised me. Not the question itself, but that Gabriel had thought enough to ask it.

"Not especially," I replied. "There are things you might have asked me to do that I would have refused as reprehensible. To be honest, delivering questionable cargo is probably low on the spectrum of dangerous errands you could have had me running." I rolled my shoulders to get the stiffness of being cramped up in the cab of my truck all day out of my body. "You gave me information, and I owed you a favor. I'm a man of my word."

"As am I," Gabriel said as he counted the money I had given him, along with the list of clients I had visited that day, and wrote everything down in a leather-bound ledger on the desk in front of him. I had no idea what was in the cases and packages I delivered today, and I had zero interest in finding out. The less I knew, the better when it came to the Lilith Nest.

"If we're finished, then I'll take my leave." I'd been gone all day and had already missed River, but that didn't mean I wanted to hang around all evening, too. Conversation with Gabriel was awkward and exhausting.

"Just a moment." Gabriel looked up from his figures, counted out a sum of money, and handed it to me. I took it without thinking, but my surprise must have shown on my face. "The requirement was doing the job for me today. I needed you to do it; I didn't need you to do it for free."

"Are you a good guy in disguise, Gabriel?" I pocketed the money. I had expected that the favor was doing his running for free, but I would not turn down cash I had earned, no matter who offered it.

"I don't labor under those types of notions, Jonas. I'm a businessman, nothing more and nothing less. I also might feel a little guilty about ruining your evening last night. I didn't intend to start a fight, and I get the distinct feeling your Miss McNee doesn't like me."

Well, that was news. "I highly doubt you feel any definition of bad over your behavior last night. And I don't think it's a dislike as much as fear. You're a vampire, Gabriel. That's scary, you know? Plus you know much more about her situation than anyone not on the Court should. She already hates her powers, and finding out that other people know about them is probably disconcerting."

"True," Gabriel admitted. "But I like being scary. Fear is a marvelous motivator. And I find River and her power very interesting indeed. Such a pity she isn't using it to her full potential."

"Why are you so interested in River?" I wasn't afraid of Gabriel, but I didn't want him focusing on my girl, either. Viktor may have been the head of the Lilith nest of vampires, but when he was away, Gabriel was number one, and he had an entire army of vampire underlings at his disposal. They weren't a threat to me. The same couldn't be said of River.

"Flames. Chaos. Destruction. The vision Rodavan had was of River killing herself with her own fire. The entire scene was nothing but River in agony, voices screaming, and the crackling of the all-encompassing flames. Tell me, what isn't fascinating about that? A beautiful woman wielding a terrible power—it's an intoxicating thought."

"You're a pervert, and we aren't talking about River now. We're talking about what happened when she was a child," I admonished.

Gabriel tugged at the sleeves of his perfectly pressed white shirt, the only indication he was becoming irritated with my questioning. Gabriel didn't like being questioned. Gabriel was the type of man used to being obeyed, not challenged. I didn't give a damn.

"From what I can tell, the Court had nothing to do with River being raised outside of town at all; that was all the McNees getting wound up at the way Rodavan treated them when they brought River to Havenwood Falls. Not that I blame them. I can't stand the Bishops. The best the Court could do was allowing the sisters to raise her, not within the town itself, but still within the protection of the wards."

"You mean still within the wards so they could keep an eye on her, right?" I was seeing how things had unfolded. I'd always wondered why the Court would order someone outside of the town but still inside the wards. It didn't seem like something they would do. In Havenwood Falls, either you were in or you were so far out you didn't remember the town existed.

"Who knows what they were thinking?" Gabriel said, as he moved along the office wall and studied the books that lined it on the right side. "But I'm not on the Court, not that I give a damn what they do, and I'm not the one who made those decisions. She doesn't live inside Havenwood Falls, and she has no reason to, unless you plan on giving her one?"

Some feral part of me growled in irritation. Not so much because Gabriel suggested it, more so because it reminded me of how the evening had turned out. "Not likely, at least not anytime soon. Not that it isn't my end game. I had a setback."

I didn't know why I was even discussing this with him. This was the longest exchange of words I'd ever had with the man, and I was sure he had some ulterior motive for even talking to me. There was always an ulterior motive.

"Yes, your smoke show in the alley. What a pitiful display."

He had to be joking. He saw the whole thing? Was he spying on us?

"I didn't know voyeurism was your thing, Gabriel."

"I was observing, Jonas. Trust me, I'm not a Peeping Tom, and even if I was, my interests run more exotic than sneaking around in alleys at night. I'm curious about River's powers and the extent she goes through to repress them. I wasn't aware that you would be groping each other the minute you thought you were alone." Gabriel paused and laughed under his breath—a deep, knowing chuckle that raised the hair on the back of my neck. Repressing the urge to punch him in the face was becoming more and more difficult, but I needed Gabriel, and he knew it. "She lit you on fire, Jonas. I think that's concerning for your future, don't you think?"

"You think this is funny, Gabriel? Because I don't. This is frustrating, and I want to help her, but she keeps pushing me away."

"Well, someone had better help her." Gabriel was all business again. "The vision that the Court had—it still stands."

"And?" I prodded, irritated that he was drawing this out. I also wondered how he had come by this information. The Court was tight-lipped about anything that went on in their proceedings. Gabriel must have been a mind reader to glean that sort of information.

"And it was the same thing. Flames. Chaos. Destruction. River has hated and suppressed her power for so long. She's ignored it, tried to act like it isn't a part of her very being. What happens when you deny yourself, Jonas, your very soul? You poison yourself. She will destroy herself simply because she knows no better. What a waste." Gabriel shook his head as if he couldn't understand the folly of youth.

"How do you know all this? Why do you care?" It made little sense. I didn't like having Gabriel's focus on River. Not for any amount of time.

"Does it matter why I care? The point is she's dangerous. To herself and others. That is an undeniable fact. The Court saw it then, and you can deny it all you want, but you are seeing it too. Hell, even River knows. Why do you think she keeps pushing you away?" Gabriel's tone was heated, his eyes a swirling storm of blue as he gave his passionate dialogue. He was more than likely right, but his timing was suspect. Why talk to me about this? Why now?

"Something will happen soon," he continued. Almost as if he had read my mind. I knew he couldn't, though. That wasn't his bread and butter. Old Man Elsmed was the one who could read thoughts.

"Old Man Elsmed isn't the only one. Some of us hold our cards a little closer to our chest."

That explained a lot, but at the same time, opened the door for a lot more questions.

"That's a nasty little secret to keep hidden, Gabriel." I held my breath and tried to keep my mind as blank as possible. With as many times as I had mentally punched him in the face, I didn't want to think about him knowing I had been imagining it.

He rolled his eyes in an uncharacteristic look of exasperation. "Relax. It's not something I enjoy. It's a little curse I picked up during a scuffle in New Orleans a while back."

Gabriel was an immortal vampire; a while back could cover a lot of ground.

"A scuffle?" What the hell kind of scuffle ends in a curse?

"Let's just say the reason Viktor is gone right now and I'm here is because my presence in New Orleans would make his negotiations . . . difficult."

"You mean you aren't allowed back there?" I smirked, but he acted like he didn't see it.

"Do you think you have the luxury of time to pick apart my past? I've lived more lifetimes than you could dream of. Perhaps you should switch your focus back to your damsel and her imminent danger. Because she is, you know." Gabriel arched his perfect dark eyebrows and picked at an imaginary piece of lint on his sleeve. "In danger."

My blood turned to ice in my veins. "How do you know?"

"There are two new humans in town. No powers. But one of them . . . he's got a dark soul. Some real nasty thoughts, that one. And there's a connection to River, though they aren't here for her. I think if they run into each other, it could be bad."

"What kind of bad?"

"Flames. Chaos. Destruction."

"Why are you so damn cryptic all the time? Spell it out for me, dammit." One should know better than to cross swords or words with a vampire who had a short temper like Gabriel, and I was probably using up whatever good luck I had, but damn if he wasn't a frustrating man. "And for someone who just told me you don't read thoughts regularly, you are *frightfully* in the know about all kinds of urgent business."

Ignoring me as if my insult was beneath his notice, Gabriel pulled a book off the shelf. The cover was deep hunter green, and the binding was cracked and worn. It looked to be a well-used book, and I didn't believe he had just magically plucked it from its place by accident. He knew damn well what he had been looking for. Just like he enjoyed feeding me important information piece by agonizing piece, everything was a production to Gabriel Doyle. Everything was a dramatic power trip. He'd probably been waiting for this exact moment, to pull his prize out with a flourish. *Bastard.* I didn't even bother trying to hide the thought; I hoped he heard it.

Turns out, the book wasn't a book at all, but a hollowed-out box made to look like one. He opened the lid and paused. "Let me ask you this before I go any further," he said, his voice heavy with warning. "How far are you willing to go to save River McNee?"

I didn't question how he knew what he did. Nor did I think for even a minute he was offering me information out of the goodness of his heart. He was dangling the bait before me, his lips curved into the smile of a man who knew he had the hook embedded deeply enough, he could reel in as slow as he liked; there was no danger of losing the prize. He wanted to know how far I would go for River? He didn't even have to ask. If he read minds, then he already knew the answer.

I looked him dead in the eyes. "I'll go as far as it takes, and then I'll go ten steps farther. What's in the book?"

CHAPTER 10

RIVER

I'd made good on my promise to myself not to breathe a word to the sisters. I'd packed my side cart like I always did, and if I left for town several hours earlier than I normally would, no one thought anything was amiss. They probably thought I would spend more time with Jonas. They didn't know what happened between us. Hell, I didn't know if I could explain it to them if I wanted to. I was what happened between us. Me. I'd broken us before we could even be together. I wasn't fit for him. He deserved someone better. Someone stronger. Someone less *flammable*.

But I couldn't worry about that now. I had to deal with Wesa—*sorry*, Thomas—and Mr. Weisman being in Havenwood Falls. I had to convince them both that there was a normal explanation for how I came to be here. They couldn't know, or even question the normalcy of this town. If I told them about all of the supernatural creatures, or the magic of the falls themselves, that would be a one-way ticket to banishment. Even the Sisters McNee couldn't save me from that.

Per our agreement, I met Thomas in the same place we met the day before, and as I parked the motorbike next to the schoolyard, he came walking around the corner. I had to admit, he cut a fine figure in his brown britches and pale blue cotton shirt, sleeves rolled up to the elbows. He wore no hat, and I saw that he kept his dark hair short, as was the fashion these days. He smiled when he saw me, and it lit up his whole face. The jagged scar on his chin did nothing to take away from the handsomeness of his strong, angular features.

He's handsome, but he looks nothing like my Jonas.

Where that thought came from, I didn't know, but I had no business comparing the two men. It wasn't fair to either of them, and I had no intention of dallying with either. Thinking of him as *my* Jonas was part of how I got in bad shape to begin with. I looked behind Thomas, but didn't see a vehicle.

"Where's your car?" I also wondered where he had left Mr. Weisman.

"Hank has the car today. I don't need it. I walked here from the inn and left him to his own devices today. You can leave your motorcycle here if you like—I thought maybe we could go exploring? I did some walking about here yesterday afternoon and found a mountain path I'd like to check out."

Exploring? He wanted to hike? I hadn't expected that, and here I was, in another one of my long skirts and wearing a pair of soft-soled shoes, similar to slippers. He must have seen the look on my face, and looking to see where my gaze landed, he laughed.

"Still hate wearing hard-soled shoes, River? It's nice to see not everything about you has changed." He laughed again and offered me his arm. "Relax, River, I'm not asking you to forge a road through the thickening forest. I won't let you ruin your dress or your shoes. I want to walk with you, and have a private discussion while doing it. I would imagine the things we'll talk about are probably words you don't want others to overhear?"

He said it lightly, but I didn't miss the implication. He wouldn't be so easy to redirect with talks about two kindly old ladies who stumbled upon me in the forest and adopted me on the spot. Thomas wanted answers. The kind only I could give. He was right; privacy was our best option.

I had to admit the walk was nice, even if the path he found was more like a faded, hardened dirt line barely big enough for two people to walk across. The foliage had already taken over, and I imagined it was an old hunting trail we were treading on, unused for some time, if the state of the grass growing over it was any sign. But the conversation was pleasant, and Thomas was quick to grab my arm and hold me steady on the occasion I snagged my shoe on an errant root.

"I've lived in this area for the last sixteen years, and I've never been up this patch of mountain," I told Thomas, looking around nervously. I would hate for either of us to get lost, especially with him being a visitor, of all things.

"Don't worry, River. I walked this yesterday. There's a hunting cabin not far up ahead. I don't know that anyone's used it in a while, but it's clean enough. We can have our conversation there."

"That's a lot of prep work just for a conversation."

I hadn't meant it to sound like an accusation, but once the words were out, the implication was clear enough. Thomas stopped walking and put his hand on my arm, and I had no choice but to stop walking and face him. His eyes were dark and serious, and I couldn't handle the emotion swimming in their depths, so I focused on his chin instead.

"River. Hank Weisman is a tired old man now, but he wasn't always that way, and I'm not so old myself that I don't remember what happened in the schoolyard all those years ago. I *know* what I saw. And I know that in the years since, Hank told me all about the storeroom he locked you in and the plans the Cranes had for you. He might not have been there for it, but he knew what they would do, and the guilt of it has eaten away at his mind ever since. He also told me some things the Cranes were ranting about when they came back that night. They told everyone you ran away and died in the woods. They used you as a deterrent for any of the rest of us to get out of line. That what happened to you is what would happen to any of the other kids who thought of running away. Hank assumed they killed you. We now know that isn't the case, so I'd like to know what happened, and I imagine you want no one overhearing when you tell me."

He spoke with the authority of a man who was used to getting what he wanted; even though his earlier words had hinted at a depth of persecution I had blessedly been spared. I smiled and walked again. "You've become a man now, haven't you, Thomas?"

"Good of you to notice." He returned my smile, picking up the pace until he was walking ahead of me. "Just a few more moments, and we'll be there. I'll race you, if you think you can catch me."

"I can't and let's not," I said, laughing at his happy face. *Ah, Wesa . . . no matter what name you go by now, it's so good to see your smile.*

"I think I see why no one comes up to this place anymore," I whispered nervously as I took in the ramshackle outbuilding. While the walls seemed sturdy enough, the ground beneath it was another story. Whether from years of washout and erosion, or another reason I hadn't thought about, the ground to the side of the cabin plummeted, revealing a drop of fifty feet at least before angling down into the rocky plains below.

"Thomas, that cabin is two big bad wolf breaths away from being blown right down the side of this mountain."

"Nonsense. I was just in there yesterday. It's perfectly stable." Thomas smiled with a wicked glint in his eyes. "It would take four breaths at least before we slid to our doom."

"I'll stay outside of it, all the same." I couldn't help but smile with him. "We're far enough away from prying ears this far up, I would think, anyway." I found a fallen log, worn over on the ends from time and nature, and sat on it, smoothing my skirt down over my legs. Thomas took a seat on a large flat stone that sat high out of the ground nearby.

"Can you tell me your story, River? We suffered so much when you were gone. How did you get away?"

"Before I tell you, can I ask you how you came to be traveling with Mr. Weisman? It was a shock to see you after all these years . . . and together even. My last memory of him wasn't so pleasant, so I'm not sure of what kind of man he turned out to be that you would still be with him after all this time."

Thomas looked at me and smiled. "You know, it was only a school, not a prison." His head hung low, and his shirt strained against his shoulders as he rested his elbows on his knees. "Everyone got to go home to their parents when their schooling was through, but me? I couldn't do it. I was too different, too changed. I never went back."

I didn't understand. What did he mean, he never went back? I asked him as much.

"I mean, I never went home. The Cranes passed probably seven years after you left, and they brought in new teachers. I had learned everything they would teach me, and it came time to go home to my parents. I couldn't do it. Hank had mentioned taking a teaching position at another school—I don't know, I think the memories were terrible for him too, so he asked me if I wanted to go with him. Maybe he felt guilty for turning his back on all the nasty things the Cranes did to us kids. To me. To you. I don't know. But he adopted me, and I have his last name, and it's been the two of us ever since. Hank is too old and infirm to teach anymore, so our roles are reversed now. I do the teaching and take care of him. He's the one who found the advertisement for the teaching positions in Colorado and brought it to my attention. It's sheer coincidence that one of them happened to be in Havenwood Falls. This place is out in the middle of nowhere. I'm surprised we could find it at all. I would imagine the winters are difficult to navigate."

I would imagine the winter would be impossible for you to navigate, I thought to myself, keeping my face schooled and impassive. Havenwood Falls was secluded by design. The only people that made it to us were the people we wanted here. Even so, the serendipity of our situation still amazed me.

"You know, I was just a small boy when I saw you last, River," Thomas continued, his eyes dark and serious. "But I still remember like it was yesterday. I still see it in my dreams. I remember the air got hot, and the ground beneath me, too. I wanted to get up and run away, but I couldn't. I'm ashamed to say I was afraid. You were so angry, and your hair had pulled out of your braids somehow and was floating around your shoulders all wild and bright. You looked like a devil or a god, I couldn't tell which. Afterwards, they said it'd been a trick you did, something with kerosene, but I know the truth. When you opened your mouth and spit the fire . . . how did you do that?"

Our eyes met while I considered how to answer him. Did I tell the truth or a half truth? How much of me would Thomas be able to handle?

"I don't know how I did it," I answered truthfully. "I was just so angry, I couldn't keep it inside anymore." I tugged on the end of my braid like I always did when I was thinking. "That's how it works mostly, anyway," I whispered almost to myself. "I stuff it down, deep inside. I don't think about it until I get emotional about something, and then . . ."

"And then what? Has something else happened?" Wesa's face was a mask of concern. He was so nice, this sweet boy from the past, to be concerned over me after all this time.

"Did you know the only ones of our people that knew about me were my parents? I had to keep it under wraps all this time. Do you think the elders would have been okay with me breathing fire like someone from the stories? No, I would have been put to death."

Wesa nodded. "That was our way."

I couldn't argue with him. That *was* our way. We told the stories of our ancestors, and we worshipped our gods, but people weren't born with power like I had. I would have been seen as a threat. And that wasn't limited to just my people. The men who took us to the Carlisle school and forced their beliefs down our throats? Those same people that called us savages and beseeched us to leave our witching ways, they were the same. It was also their way. And hadn't I the invisible marks around my neck to prove it? They couldn't be seen, but those marks would never fade for me.

"So you showed no one? Never?" Thomas looked like he didn't believe me, and I guess I understood that.

"Not since I showed my mother I could burn pretty pictures into the grass when I was young. The fear in my mother's eyes . . . it was awful. She made me promise never to do it again. I was never to show anyone, because terrible things would happen if I did. Then she and father both died. After that, the soldiers came and took us all away. So I was afraid. And I didn't do it again. Not until—"

"Not until you saw me being beaten in the schoolyard." Thomas finished the sentence for me solemnly.

"We were just children. Hungry children," I cried, tears forming in the corners of my eyes as I recalled the memory. "And he was smiling, Wesa. He was smiling as he beat you and your blood was all over his hands." I'd forgotten again to call him Thomas, but he didn't correct me.

"And you haven't used it since then?"

"Not on purpose." I didn't know any other way to answer that question. I'd thought I'd buried my flames until Jonas got me all stirred up inside. Emotional. He made me feel . . . things. I couldn't explain that to Thomas. Not something that personal.

"So how did you get away from the Cranes? The story they gave Hank was fantastic, although I would imagine by the time I was old enough to hear it, some minor details may have changed. They said something about an ungodly wailing . . ."

"I don't know what to tell you about that," I said, going the cautious route and telling as simple a tale as I could. "Mr. Crane was drunk, that much I know, and they tied the sloppiest noose in the world. They tied me up high to a rotten branch that broke under my weight almost immediately. They just got spooked by something and didn't bother to check to make sure they had actually killed me. They just assumed they'd done the job." It was a lie, but I wove as much of the truth in there as I could.

"What could have spooked those two so much that they would leave without checking that you were dead? It makes little sense. How did you get out of the woods then? You were just a child, too." He was asking all of the good questions, but I'd already decided not to tell him anything that would jeopardize the sisters or Havenwood Falls.

Sorry, Thomas, I just can't.

"After I got the rope from around my neck, I ran as fast and as hard as I could in the complete opposite direction. I ran throughout the night until my legs wouldn't move anymore, and then when I thought I was just going to lie on the ground and die, I made it to a road. And passing by on that road were two women, traveling west.

They took pity on me, and finding out I had no family, let me stay with them. After all of that traveling, I ended up here in the mountains, where I've been ever since. It's not that exciting a tale, once you get past the attempted murder and danger."

His eyes were as flat as the line of his mouth. "I don't buy that story. It's a little too far-fetched."

"As far-fetched as a girl who can breathe fire and escaped being executed?"

His stare was sharp now, almost a weapon, cutting through my defensive layers and trying to find the truth revealed within. "Mrs. Crane swore it was fairies."

Oh, God, she was pretty damn close.

"Fairies?" I laughed it off. "Now who's got a far-fetched story, Thomas?"

He said nothing in reply, so I continued on, emboldened by my determination to stick to my lie. "That's what happened, and you can take it or leave it. I mean, I don't know why I could use the flames, but it isn't anything I'm proud of. It isn't anything I enjoy. And I have never met anyone else able to do so, either. I'm a freak; even our own people would have thought so. There's no safe place for me if anyone finds out, you know? Look what happened with the Cranes."

"The Cranes were awful people."

I happened to share his sentiment.

"He was an evil drunk, she was a hysterical nutter, and I'm not sorry they're dead. I'm not sorry at all." The words flew out of my mouth in a frenzy. I meant them, even though I would probably be ashamed that I'd said such a thing later. It wasn't ladylike, and Alice and Meri had always taught me not to speak ill of the dead lest you bring their sorrows upon yourself. It had sounded like suspicious nonsense at the time, but one never could be too careful.

Thomas smiled then, a slow curving of his lips that spread up his face but just didn't quite seem to reach his eyes. The breeze blew down through the trees on our side of the mountain, and the wooden walls of the tiny cabin creaked on the unsteady foundation.

"I'm so happy to hear it, River. I'm so glad you feel that way."

Thomas stood and walked toward me, stopping when our knees were almost touching, and he grabbed both of my hands in his. "I'm overjoyed right now. I'm so happy, I think I want to tell you my secret. Since you know. Since you hated them, too. They hurt you so much, just like me." Then he laughed, and it wasn't a nice laugh. It was high pitched and nasal, like it traveled through his nose instead of his throat. The jagged scar on his chin shone white against his burnished skin, and his lips stretched too wide when he grinned. "It makes me so glad I killed them."

CHAPTER 11

JONAS

*S*he wasn't there.

It wasn't like River to not show up to the mine for lunch —especially when there were orders to fill. In the last few years since she'd been catering to laborers, she had never not shown up. I could count on one hand the amount of times she'd been sick with a cold or some other ailment, and had one of the sisters' friends in town take over for the day, but that was it. Today she was a complete no-show.

The hungry men who'd climbed the grassy hill like they did every day stood in line, questioning looks on their faces. Where in the hell was River?

"I don't understand," Ian mumbled next to me. "She was here yesterday. Everything seemed fine; she even let me eat your lunch."

"Did she say anything?"

"What, you mean about you? She didn't have to. She looked like someone had kicked her puppy right in front of her. Not sure what happened between you guys, Jonas, but I told her to stop jerking you around."

He said what now?

"That's not your place," I growled low in my throat, letting the threat simmer close to the surface.

"It wasn't like that, idiot. We didn't have that type of conversation.

Besides, she looked sad that you weren't in her line, even though you said she'd be trying to avoid you."

"Even not knowing I wouldn't be here, she showed up yesterday, so why wouldn't she be here today?" I didn't have the answer, but after the discussion Gabriel and I had the day before, a sick feeling began in the pit of my stomach. This could be nothing, but since it was River, it was probably something.

"Man, I'm so hungry," Ian grumbled next to me.

"I have to go."

"What do you mean, you have to go? It's the middle of the work day. Are you going to find food somewhere? I doubt you have time for a sit-down meal right now."

"No. I mean I have to go. Right now." I didn't have time to explain to him. The feeling in my stomach was growing stronger, and I had the horrible urge to run in five directions at once. My skin itched, and I felt my transformation hovering close to the surface. I needed to find River. Now.

"Do you know what you're doing? This is your job, man."

"No, Ian," I threw over my shoulder as I jogged back down the hill toward the dirt lot where I parked my truck that morning. "It's *just* a job. She's my priority."

Two new humans in town with a connection to River, and now she didn't show up for deliveries when you could set a clock to her?

No way could I sit on that, no way.

I burst into Gabriel's study so hard, the heavy wooden doors slammed back against the wall. Heedless to the snapping and growling of the vampires who knew they couldn't even dent my skin, I blew past them so fast their hair wafted in the breeze. I had no time for politeness or pleasantries. I might have been less hasty if the master had been home, but since Viktor wasn't around and I had business with Gabriel, I allowed myself the bravery of throwing myself into the Lilith Nest.

He was expecting me. Of course he was.

Or at least it looked to be so. He was sitting with his jacket over the back of the chair and his elbows resting on the desk in front of him. In one hand he held a strange looking amulet, a black stone swinging lightly from a chain. It had no shine, no luster, but more of a flat matte finish. In his right hand was an ornate pen, which he used to write in a ledger in front of him. He was taking notes, but I couldn't be bothered to find out why. I recognized the amulet from the day before. It was the same one he'd pulled out of the book on the shelf that was not a book, but a safe to hide objects in plain sight. He'd stolen it from a voodoo woman and added it to his already long list of reasons he shouldn't return to New Orleans. I didn't care about the origins; I only cared about how it would help River.

"Something's happened to her." The words came out low and raspy. My change was close, and it was a testament to my desperation that I was having such a hard time controlling such a simple bodily function.

"No it hasn't. Not yet, anyway" was all he said in reply as he scribbled a few more notes down in his book. His indifference was infuriating, considering recent events. I slammed my hand down on the desk, the weight of my fist cracking the highly polished wood and sending his notebook and obnoxiously expensive-looking pen skittering sideways. I was a stone man, and a big one at that. Had I wanted to use my full power, I could have split that solid wood desk in half, and quite possibly the body sitting behind it, as well. But I didn't want to hurt him. I wanted his attention.

"That desk cost more than your wages can keep up with," Gabriel murmured, but the threat lacked heat.

"We can wax poetic about your prissy obsession with overpriced furniture another time," I growled. "But River didn't show up to the mine today. She's not late, and she didn't send a substitute—she's just not there. I already checked her house; the sisters said she left early this morning. Where is she, Gabriel?"

I don't know why I thought he would know, maybe because he was always so cocksure and *seemed* to know something about everything under the sun. I'd lost precious time already, running out of town to the sisters, but it seemed the obvious first place to check. I regretted upsetting them, but I had to check every option, and when I'd left, they had begged me to find their girl. To banshees, there is nothing more important than their family. Once a banshee claims you as her own, it's a most powerful bond.

"I don't know why you think I know so much about what's going on." The bastard had the nerve to smile while he said it.

"I'll have you swallow your next flippant comment, I swear it. Where is she? What do we do?"

"What is this *we* you speak of?" Gabriel asked, one finely shaped brow arched high on his aristocratic forehead. "I supply you with information, Jonas. The rest is based purely on the amount of effort you will exert for this female. Are you sure she's worth it?"

The only response I could give was a low grinding sound. My stone form would explode through my skin if he didn't change his tone.

"Gabriel," I ground out. "Where. Is. River." It wasn't even a question this time, but pure demand. Polite Jonas was about to disappear, and my feral side was not in the mood to mince words.

Gabriel sighed, like dealing with someone too thick to appreciate his prose was exhausting, and closing his fingers around the black amulet, he held it out to me. "Here, take this. You know well the cost of it, though. I'll have what I want out of this deal. I don't know exactly where she is, but I have a guess."

"You have a guess?"

"It's an educated guess," he replied. "Take the damn amulet before I change my mind and let you figure this little debacle out on your own."

I took the amulet from him and willed myself to stay composed and not punch him in the face until my fist came out the other side. My regular self was pretty nonviolent but my wild self was . . . something different.

To distract myself, I studied the small amulet in my hands. It looked plain, plainer than I would have thought coming from Gabriel, and upon closer inspection, I saw that the surface of the stone was rife with uneven pock marks.

"This is lava rock, isn't it?" I'd seen one once before from a visiting merchant. Lava rock was stone created from cooled magma that had erupted from volcanos.

"Fitting, isn't it?" Gabriel said, his composure restored and his usual mocking smile in place. "That stone can take high heat without breaking down, and with the wicked nasty juju it's infused with, this little amulet should work for our needs."

Our needs. I mustn't forget our discussion and the real reason Gabriel was helping me right now. There was always a catch. Gabriel Doyle was a shrewd businessman, after all, and this was another transaction. I'd take this deal, though, to save River, and may she not forever hate me for it.

I said I'd do whatever it takes.

Gabriel walked toward the door, swinging his jacket from the chair and around his shoulders as he went. It was much too warm for such an article of clothing on a warm summer day, even high in the mountains, but it was a fashion. And Gabriel was at all times nattily dressed.

"Are you coming?" Gabriel peered over his shoulder, as if I was the one holding up the show. "You drive; I'll tell you where to go."

"Your truck is a travesty, Pederson," Gabriel grumbled as his head hit the roof of the cab when I went over a deep groove in the road.

"I bought this truck brand new in 1921, and it's only three years old. She's perfect; she just needs some tweaking now and again." He'd better not insult my baby. I'd saved my coins like a miser to afford this truck, and I custom built the back end for cargo. Not everyone had a vehicle in Havenwood Falls, but I did.

"Tweaking?" Gabriel looked at me, incredulous. His normally put-together persona wore a mask of disbelief.

"It's practical," I shot back, as I careened too quickly around the corner toward Havenwood Falls Elementary School.

"It's barbaric is what it is." His grumble turned into a pained yelp as I slammed the brakes and his knees hit the dash. "You're crazy, Pederson!"

I didn't answer him. I was too busy staring at what had caused me to hit the brakes in the first place—River's motorbike. It was right there in front of the school. Leaving Gabriel to follow, I swung the truck door open and leapt from the vehicle.

She was here. I didn't know how he knew it, but she was here.

But she wasn't any longer. The side cart was still stocked with all of the brown-bagged lunches that never got delivered to the miners, and there was no sign of her at all. "How did you know she'd be inside the school?"

"She isn't," Gabriel said from behind me.

"Okay, where is she then?" I didn't have time for the word games he seemed to love so much.

"Shut up." Surprised, I looked at Gabriel. He had his eyes closed and his mouth drawn down in concentration. He mumbled something too low for me to hear, but he wasn't talking to me, anyway. Moving his right arm in an arc in front of him and his left in the opposite direction he stood stock still for a moment. It was if he commanded even the birds and the insects to be silent so he could hear even the faintest of sounds. Then his eyes snapped open, the irises blazing blue and focused on something only he could see. "There," he said, making an about face and pointing up the mountain side. "She's up there."

"Hell. That's going to be a hike on foot," I said, staring at the dense forest that started in the near distance and crept up in a wall of green. I wouldn't be doing it in this form, that was for sure.

Gabriel seemed to read what I was thinking. "I'll need you to at least wait until you are hidden by the tree line before you do anything drastic, Pederson. I can get away with a lot of things in this town, but I think a giant rock man charging up the mountainside at breakneck speed would be difficult to hide from the Court."

"You think that's bad? My body transforms, but my clothes do not." *Let that sink in for a moment.*

"That sounds like a personal problem." Gabriel smirked. "It must be difficult to operate under such . . . limitations."

"Do you want a fireman carry, or a princess carry?" I asked with a grin, already moving toward the cool dark of the tree line.

"Don't flatter yourself, stone man," Gabriel said as he jogged past me, a genuine grin on his face for the first time I had ever witnessed. "I'll get up this mountainside on my own. I don't need your primitive methods. Worry about yourself."

I would worry about myself. And I would worry about River. If she was in trouble, and that was most likely the case, I'd smash through anything that kept her from me. No humans from her past or River's raging flames would keep me from her side, even if I had to expose my true nature in the process.

CHAPTER 12

RIVER

*T*he odd look on Thomas's face distracted me. That was why I surely had not heard him correctly. There was no way he had said what I thought he'd said. It didn't fit.

"I'm sorry, what did you say? I think I misheard." I smiled in embarrassment.

He squeezed my hands again, this time harder than normal. "I killed the Cranes—both of them. I knew you of all people would understand. Oh, River," he sighed as he pulled me to my feet and embraced me. "I'm so happy to have found you here. It's like a gift from the gods. Surely I'm on the right path." He nuzzled his face in my neck and inhaled deeply while I stood frozen in shock.

This wasn't right. My brain couldn't keep up with the complete one-eighty turn of events, and Thomas was definitely taking physical liberties with me. Jonas had held me the same way not two days ago, but it had felt completely different.

"I don't understand." I pushed against his chest, and he stepped back, still smiling that creepy smile that didn't reach his eyes.

"You poor thing." His misplaced sympathy combined with the sudden strength of his grip on me rang warning bells throughout my entire body. What was he talking about?

"You poor, poor girl," he repeated, his hands rubbing my arms as if to comfort me. It had the opposite effect. "After all this time, you still live in fear when you hold the key to making those people all pay for what they did."

"Making who pay? For what? And what about the Cranes? Thomas, I don't understand." For lack of any better idea, and because I wanted to pull out of his weird hypnotic embrace, I sat back down on the log, while Thomas remained standing in front of me.

He smiled proudly. "They all thought she slipped in the kitchen and fell. The impact of her head hitting the iron cook stove killed her instantly, and she bled out on the floor." Thomas tilted his head like he was imparting a great secret. "While the blow killed her, she didn't slip. It was my hand that knocked her down. It wasn't an accident she hit the stove. Although if I had known it would kill her so quickly, I would have thought of something else. She ought to have suffered."

My breath caught in my throat, but no sound escaped.

"And he wasn't much better. Moping around after she died. I'd expected more sport with him, but he was so drunk all the time, it wasn't even fun, waiting until he was asleep and then propping him just right with his shotgun. That was much messier than I had expected. I had to burn my clothes." Thomas shuddered at the memory, and I didn't know what disturbed me more—that he had killed the Cranes, or that he was only disturbed by how the whole affair had damaged his clothing.

Thomas was *not* okay.

My head was spinning, and I couldn't get a grasp of the situation. "But you travel with Mr. Weisman. How could he not know?"

"I only kept that old fool alive because he was useful," Thomas sneered. His polite mask was gone, and now in its place was something twisted and ugly. "He was so riddled with guilt, he'd believe anything I said. He got me out of that school and away from that place. He'll spend the rest of his life trying to make up for turning his back on things, and even though he's about ready to keel over now, there's still use in him yet. And now that we found you—it can only get better."

The way he said those words made bile rise in my throat.

"River, aren't you angry? Don't you want to hurt the ones that hurt you?"

The ones that hurt me?

"Is that why you killed the Cranes?" I whispered. Not because I was trying to stay quiet, but because that's all the strength I had to speak. This Thomas was terrifying.

"They were nasty people, and they deserved to die. I'm glad they're dead. You said the same thing. But what about the other wrongs? The soldiers that stole us from our families—the ones that raped our lands and killed our people—shouldn't they pay, River? They should. They should all pay." Thomas nodded even though I hadn't given him a reply. He was living in a fantasy of his own making; he didn't need a response from me. In his mind, *of course* I agreed with him. There was no need to confirm this.

"With your flames, we could destroy armies, River."

"No." Just one word, but I made it firm.

"Hmm?" He wasn't even listening.

"No, I won't do that. I won't hurt anyone. I think you're sick, Thomas, and my heart hurts for the things that have happened to you, but I won't use my power to hurt anyone. Ever." There were a few seconds of silence as my words sunk in, and then the world tipped upside down.

"Why not?" The words erupted from his mouth in the first real anger he had shown, and the slap across my face came so hard and so fast, it knocked me clean off the stump I sat on. I flew backward into the dirt, my head hitting the hard packed-dirt ground and my skirts getting tangled in my legs.

You've got to get away from him.

"River," Thomas said as he stood over me, one leg on each side of my body caging me in. "I don't want to force you. I mean I will, and I'm going to." He laughed as he grabbed the front of my blouse and flung me to my feet, catching me in his cruel grasp. "I wish you could see things from my eyes. We could have everything."

"Your eyes are clouded, Wesa," I said, saying his true name with a gasp as one of his hands wound its way through one thick braid and yanked. I gritted my teeth and pressed on. "What would your parents think?"

"My parents? What about them? They let the soldiers take me away. They never even tried to come get me. Why would I care about them? I wonder if they're dead now," he mused, never letting go of me.

"Let me go," I pleaded. I needed to think of a plan, but in the meantime I also needed to keep him talking. "I don't want to use my power to hurt people, and you can't make me."

This time I saw the blow coming, but I still couldn't block it, and the force of his fist on the side of my head took my vision and my breath all at the same time. Pain exploded through my body, and the urge to vomit was severe. He threw me to the ground with a thud, and I lacked the strength to right myself. A thin stream of blood ran from my nose, down my lip, and plopped into the dirt.

"I can make you do anything, River. It's a matter of finding the right motivation." Thomas laughed again, and this time I gave in to the urge, retching into the dirt until my stomach was empty. Wiping my nose and mouth on my sleeve, I glared up at him. My vision was still blurry from the blow to my head, and he wavered in front of me like a mirage.

"I won't give you my fire."

"You don't have to give me anything. I'll take what I want, like I always have."

"Not likely, you criminal." I was hurting and having problems seeing straight. He probably thought he could beat me into doing what he wanted, and if that was the case, he would be disappointed. It wasn't *my* pain I was afraid of. It never had been.

"I think I have you figured out now, and you're so easy, it's laughable. You care too much about others, River. That's your weakness, and it's what I will use to make you my tool." He grinned again, all tan skin and white teeth, the scar on his chin a macabre reminder of the violence he'd endured to become this way.

"I'm a schoolteacher, River. How many kids' mysterious deaths would it take for you to come to heel? One? Two? An entire classroom? Let me know, and I can get started. Or you can just give me what I

want, and we both leave Havenwood Falls exactly like we found it."
He crouched down in front of me so that our eyes were level, and it
took everything in me not to cower away from him in fear. "Say the
word, and I'll get started. I'm amenable to whatever."

God, he was sick. I'd been so stupid.

"You're crazy, you know that?" I spit in his face, and he laughed.

The boot to my shoulder knocked me on my back, and I didn't
even try to get up.

"You're the one who went walking deep in the woods with a
complete stranger, little girl," he said in a singsong voice, as he walked
a tight circle around where I lay in the dirt, my whole body racked
with the pain of his earlier blows. My head still wasn't right. There was
a rhythmic thumping noise coming from the ground under me. Like a
pack of wild horses was thundering up the mountainside, hurrying to
get to the top. I was addled, there were no horses, and I was surely
imagining the ground moving underneath me.

"This town isn't what you think it is," I said, not even bothering to
open my eyes, considering I couldn't see straight, anyway. "You won't
get away with anything like what you're planning so easily. Whatever
you do, it'll be found out. And your punishment will be severe." I was
dead serious. The Court of the Sun and the Moon did not mess
around with outsiders who sought to wreak havoc in their refuge.

"Oh, I won't do anything to *you*, River. I need you." Thomas
stepped away from me and looked off in the distance, over the space
where the tree line ended and the unseen town stretched out below.
"But those two ladies who adopted you. What about them? It
shouldn't take too much digging to figure out who they are, and then I
can have fun. What was it you mentioned about your flames going out
of control? Emotional stimuli? I can make you bathe in their blood,
River. Would that encourage you to lend me your flames?"

My aunties?

The change took over so fast, I was on my feet before my eyes were
even open, the familiar sizzle in the air zipping through my skin and
out through my fingertips and the soles of my feet. The feeling was
rage. I was angry.

"You'll never come close to them," I shouted, and with my words came a stream of heat. I flung my arms in the air without thinking, and the force of my rage emerged from my fingertips in a stream of flame, right into the ramshackle cabin perched on the edge of the eroded cliff. The old and rotted wood absorbed the blast like a sponge absorbed water, and the flames ate away at the walls until the entire structure was nothing but a sea of red and orange.

"No." Horror at what I'd done froze me in place, but Thomas just laughed wildly, clapping his hands together with glee.

"See? You can do it if you put your mind to it, River. Doesn't it feel good? Doesn't it feel amazing to destroy? Come with me, and let's punish them all. Everyone who took from us. Everyone who hurt us. Let's burn it all to the ground."

I didn't want this. I didn't mean to. The more agitated and scared I got, the more the flames licked the ground in front of me. The surrounding air both crackled and spit in defiance, and I couldn't pull it back inside me if I tried. My arms and legs were awash with that burning energy, and if I tried to shake it away, I would paint the scenery in a savage inferno. Forget Thomas. I was the most dangerous being on this mountain. And he wanted to use me as a weapon.

"You won't get what you want."

"But I already have, River. I already have you, and I'll destroy everything and everyone you love to keep you." Thomas's face was a distortion, a twisted mask of cruelty. I didn't recognize this man, but I knew one thing. I had helped create him. I set everything in motion that day sixteen years ago; this was my fault.

All I ever did was hurt people. Wesa . . . Jonas . . . and now the sisters and countless residents of Havenwood Falls would be in danger, just because he wanted me.

Me.

I was the common denominator.

I was the answer and the formula for the equation. To fix this, to make sure that no one else suffered because of me, I needed to remove myself from the picture.

They would mourn, but it was the only way to make sure I never used my power to hurt anyone again. And I was so tired of fighting myself. Of suppressing the power that manifested at the most inconvenient moments.

The air shook with a boom, and something inside the burning shack exploded, probably a leftover can of kerosene or an oil lamp. Taking advantage of the distraction, I looked around as the heat of my body caused the ground to blister in front of me. I took a step toward the slope, where the foundation of dirt crumbled into a sheer drop. Twenty feet to the edge and then fifty feet down.

The sisters had taught me you should never take life lightly. They would be sad when I was gone, I knew. Tears trickled from my eyes and evaporated instantly, the heat of my skin causing them to disappear in a puff of vaporous smoke. Wesa observed the burning cabin absently, and I took five more steps toward the edge of the cliff, willing myself not to lose heart. My clothes were burning now; I wondered how long they would last. It didn't matter anymore.

It was a coward's way out, and I was about to take it, but I didn't know what else to do. If I died, no more flames would come from my body, and Wesa would have no weapon to wield. The sisters would wail. I knew they would be heard all the way into town and up the surrounding mountains.

"I'm sorry," I whispered into the wind. To the sisters and to Jonas, the man I felt so much for. But my feelings were a curse, just like my flames, and I would take them both over the side of this cliff with me.

"What do you think you're doing?" Wesa, his attention no longer occupied by the burning cabin, now stared at me with growing alarm. "Get away from there, River. I won't let you do whatever silly thing it is you're thinking." He walked toward me, and I was awash with a new emotion. Disgust.

Wesa was a bad man.

Taking a deep breath, I reached out to the flames, sucking them away from the burning foliage, away from the rickety cabin that was almost razed to the ground. I filled my lungs and my body with every bit of fire that had been expunged, and I held it inside me. It filled my veins and my organs, burning inside, twisting and turning and begging for release.

I didn't know I could do that, but then again, I'd never tried.

But the flames didn't want to stay inside me. They wanted release. They'd had a brief taste of freedom, and I was too distraught to keep them contained. They would come out of me, one way or another. That was okay, though. They would come out in a place where they couldn't hurt anyone ever again.

Wesa picked up the pace as I inched closer to the edge. I wasn't afraid now. It was he who showed his fear as the toy he'd wanted was about to disappear forever out of his reach. I would wait a couple seconds for him to come closer. I'd already realized I would never be successful at suppressing this terrible power. Hadn't I proved it by losing control and creating a circle of destruction right in front of me? *Again?* I wasn't a scared little girl anymore, tearfully promising a panel of Court members I would be good. That I wouldn't use my power again. That I would never hurt anyone. It was only a matter of time before our actions on the mountainside alerted the Luna Coven, and then the Court, of exactly what was happening. There would be no saving me from them. I'd broken my promise, and not even the sisters could step in on my behalf this time.

But I could do one last thing to make it right. To keep this damaged man in front of me from ever harming another soul ever again. I could do this *one thing right*.

"River, stop."

I wanted to say "Make me," but I couldn't. I couldn't open my mouth because the flames I'd sucked back into my body beat against my teeth and tongue, demanding release. I just needed him to get a little closer. My vision swam with the effort it cost to wrestle the demons inside me—the ones burning at my insides and fighting to be free. Through the haze of smoke, I saw a figure, large and imposing, break through the tree line and come charging into the clearing with a roar.

"River, no." I don't how I understood the words, garbled and deep. Maybe it was just a testament to how much of my mind I had lost in this battle that I was imagining it was Jonas wishing me a final farewell. I wanted to call his name, but again, to let it slip past my lips would invite disaster, and I was having a hard enough time keeping it at bay. Wesa was almost to me, and I reached out to grab his arm, flinging myself back. The weight of my body would send us both plummeting over the edge and wipe us both from this existence.

But that was not to be.

Wesa was snatched backward out of my grasp, and he went hurtling through the air, a boneless rag doll with arms and legs flailing. I didn't see where he landed, because my body was also yanked forward, away from the ledge, and I was crushed up against a wall of solid rock. Wider than I was and taller, with two massive arms of stone circled around me, the wall closed in. The roar of the flames pounded in my ears, and at last I had reached my physical limit. As two massive hands, gentle despite being made of solid stone, caressed my back, I lost the battle with my self-control.

And weeping for all of the things I would lose, I opened my mouth.

CHAPTER 13

JONAS

*W*e would not make it. I saw the smoke rising above the trees and heard the explosion a scant second later. Stripping my shirt and my pants as I ran, I let the change take me as skin and bone swelled and hardened into solid stone. My footsteps, once light and soundless, now thundered as I heaved my massive bulk up the overgrown pass, feet leaving large craters in the dirt.

"Wait a second," Gabriel drawled from behind me, keeping pace with me and not looking the least bit winded. "Take this too, you thick-headed fool." I saw the lava rock amulet dangling in his fist.

I'd almost forgotten the key.

"Are you sure you don't want me to carry you?" The words came out in a booming groan. Speaking was hard when your face was solid rock.

"There's no sense in me wasting the effort on running if you are. You'll get there faster, and you don't need me." Gabriel straightened his jacket, which had been flapping around him while we had run for the tree line. Well, I had run. I didn't see Gabriel moving. He appeared where I was when I had the thought to look for him. Vampires had many tricks up their sleeves.

He was right. He wasn't involved in this any more than a simple business transaction. It was up to me to take care of what needed done.

"Then hold these. I'll need them later," I said, and tossed my shirt and pants over my shoulder.

"Rude." Gabriel could complain all he wanted, but I couldn't wait any longer, and I took off as fast as my massive stone legs could take me. Speed wasn't a strong point in this form, but my size tripled as a stone man, and my longer stride ate up the distance between me and the place up the mountain that Gabriel had pointed to earlier. The place that was now marked with a thin plume of rising smoke.

I had to get there.

Stealth was not a skill I owned as a stone man, and the ground shook under my feet as I thundered up the path, snapping branches and sometimes even whole trees. Normally I took more care when in this form, but now time was not my friend. I couldn't count on the element of surprise, and I didn't know what I would find when I got to where I was going. I didn't even know where that was. I followed the smoke.

When I got to the source of the smoke, I almost couldn't believe my eyes. It looked to be the scene of a devastating fire, but there were no flames anywhere, even though I could smell fresh ash in the air. River stood on the edge of a steep drop, her hair a tangled mess pulled free from her braids, and her eyes were wild. They were solid black—no white showing at all—and the entire side of her face was red and purple, her lip and nose swollen and bleeding. Just steps in front of her stood a man I'd never seen before, but here he was approaching River with his arms outstretched. Her eyes stared ahead at him, seeing nothing but his face.

In a split second, I understood what she was trying to do—and I was having none of it.

"River, no!" I roared the words, but I'm sure it sounded like nothing more than the booming of thunder, and she didn't even acknowledge she heard me. She grasped the wrist of the man in front of her and reared back, shuffling her feet backward to launch them both over the sheer drop below.

Like hell.

I plucked the man right out of her grasp with one hand and tossed him over my shoulder. I didn't check to see where he landed, and I didn't care. I could deal with him later. I would rip his arms clean from his body for daring to lay a hand on River. My main target was in front of me, about to throw her life and our love away as she hurtled to her death for some self-sacrificing notion. Whatever her reasoning, it wasn't good enough, but I would let her tell me all about it later, when I knew she was safe and the black madness had bled from her eyes.

I reached her as her foot met the space where the eroded ground gave way to empty air, and instead of falling backward down the drop-off, I yanked her forward and spun her around, putting my large, immovable form between her and certain death. She couldn't go. I wouldn't let her. Even if it meant scaring her with my ugly form, I would hold her still and not let her go. I curled around her as best as I could, stroking her back as gently as was possible with my giant hands carved from stone. She turned her face up, her eyes still black and unseeing—and then she opened her mouth.

If I were a smaller man, and not a fifteen-foot-tall rock monster, I might have been bowled over by the blast. Instead, I took it full in the face, letting the heat of her rage surround me until I was nothing more than a glowing ball of flame, holding a smaller, hotter ball of flame. A human kiln, she baked me, firing my entire being until the surrounding grass burned to nothing and the soil dried out and cracked under our bodies. And still she burned. And still I held her tighter.

I could feel the heat, but it was nothing more than the heat of opening an oven and pulling out the dishes inside. I was a man of stone, and fire could not hurt me.

And still she burned.

But then, when I thought we might burn forever and would remain that way until the end of time, I felt something else— something different. The amulet I still had clasped in the cage of my fingers burned as well, but instead of disappearing into the flames, it called to them, coaxing the light into its matte mottled darkness.

And if that wasn't a strange enough sight to behold, the flames flowed into the amulet. Just like Gabriel had said they would. Soundlessly, they streamed from River's mouth, over our bodies, and into the amulet. On a current of their own, they traveled continuously into the depths of a stone that had no bottom. I don't know how long I knelt there, waiting for the flames to cease—forever or maybe just a moment. It was impossible to tell. There was no lessening of power, no gradual decrease of fire. It was there, and then it was gone, leaving River hanging limply in my arms, her eyes and mouth now closed, her chest heaving from her efforts. I was so close to the edge of the cliff my heels hung over the side where I knelt. One false move, and I would plummet to the bottom.

But the amulet had worked. River lived.

I had no way of knowing if there would be a second outburst. Gabriel had told me before that the spell that had been placed on the amulet was strong, and that if used correctly should suck in not only her flames, but the source of her power, leaving her with nothing left.

But had it worked?

I couldn't take the chance and release my stone form. It was the only defense I had against River's flames. I also didn't want to scare her, looking as I did, but holding her still was all I could think to do. So I knelt there, on the crumbling earth at the edge of a precipice, holding her until she returned to herself. Until she returned to me.

"Jonas?" Her voice quivered after what seemed like an eternity of silence.

"Don't be afraid." I said the words as quietly and as gently as I could, but the sound still reverberated off the surrounding trees.

As she lifted her head, I could see the black had bled away, and there were her big beautiful brown eyes staring at me—the eyes I loved —although one had a bluish tinge growing underneath it that sparked rage in my soul, and the glassy sheen of unshed tears slid across the surface.

"So this is the part you've kept hidden?" Her question was muffled as she dipped her head again, not meeting my eyes.

"Please don't be afraid," I repeated in the same growling voice.

"I could never be afraid of you, Jonas. Never. Where's Wesa?"

I lifted her chin with one massive finger until she met my eyes. "Is he the man that struck you? If so, he's in a pile behind you, and if he moves, I'll stomp him until he becomes one with the dirt he's lying on." That man was the least of her problems. There was something else she hadn't noticed yet, something that had happened while we had been sitting there, huddled together in the dirt. It would be an issue when she did.

I let go of her chin, and her eyes traveled up my body, taking in my mountainous form. The fingers of her right hand reached up to trace the hardness of my jaw. I barely felt her touch, soft as a butterfly's wings on the side of my face.

"Can I touch you?" she asked in wonder.

"Love, you're touching me now." And I smiled. It was grotesque, a stone ogre's grin, but I couldn't stop the expression. She gave me such joy by wanting to put her hands, even the smallest bit, on me in this formidable body.

Slowly, her gaze traveled down from my face to the wide expanse of my chest, lower still to my abdomen, and then even lower. I heard the gasp as she saw the entirety of me laid bare. When I took my stone form, my size tripled. That included *every* part.

"Jonas," River shrieked, the sound cutting through the stillness of the forest. "You're naked!"

"But River, so are you."

Her arms shot out in embarrassment, and she pushed me away, her hands splaying over the breasts she hadn't known until that moment were bare. And I watched her face go from embarrassment to horror as I slid backwards, over the edge of the cliff and down the side, cutting through the air like a lead weight as the ground rushed up to meet me with all the subtlety of a sledgehammer.

She'd pushed me off the cliff.

CHAPTER 14

RIVER

I'd pushed him off a cliff.

Jonas Pederson, a stone man in full glory, had bounded up the side of the mountain and saved me from certain death. And I returned that favor by getting embarrassed and pushing him off a cliff.

I thought I'd killed him.

But, as I knelt on the ledge barely far enough away to be safe, my head in my hands and weeping over the loss, I felt something settling over my shoulders. Startled out of my mourning, I lifted my head to see Gabriel Doyle calmly placing what looked to be one of Jonas's button-down shirts around my shoulders. I clutched the ends together over my naked body and sniffed. Yes, it was Jonas's. It smelled just like him, a mixture of woodsy outdoors, sawdust, and soap. None of those things by themselves were anything special, but together they were uniquely him. My tears began anew.

Gabriel took no notice of my naked form other than to cover it, and ambling over to the edge of the drop off, he looked over and whistled.

"That's a bit of a fall," he said to me, before turning and yelling over the side. "Pederson, we had a deal."

I don't know if he was waiting for some response, but a few seconds passed before he shook his head and grimaced.

"Oh, all right," he mumbled to himself, and I watched in silent stupor as he walked past me, retrieved a pair of pants from the grass, and walking back over to the edge, pitched them down the cliff side.

I'd fainted and was a prisoner of some sort of madness. That was the only explanation that made sense.

Gabriel stood there for a minute, staring down at what had to be Jonas's mangled body before something came hurtling through the air from down below. Gabriel caught it in his right hand, snatching it right out of the sky. I didn't know what it was, but it was attached to a slim silver chain—I saw the end of it dangling from his fist.

"Thanks, partner," he said and turned his head once more to look at whatever mess had been left on the forest floor below. "Are you coming, then?"

He wasn't talking to me.

There was no way Jonas was all right, was there?

Throwing his hands in the air in the perfect representation of complete exasperation, he sighed.

"Turn around," he said, his face serious.

"What?" I wasn't following.

"Turn. Around." He raised one finger in the air and gave it a twirling motion. "The last time you got a look at him without clothes on, you pushed him down a cliff. Your knight in stone armor isn't coming back until you turn around." Gabriel made a shooing motion with his hands, like he was ushering a naughty child out of the kitchen. "And you might want to close those buttons while you're at it, not that I'm opposed to the view." And then the heathen had the gall to wink at me.

With a gasp, I realized my state of undress, although to my credit, I had just had a traumatizing experience. I put my back to Gabriel Doyle as I fumbled with the buttons on the borrowed shirt. It was four sizes too large and covered me from my neck to my knees.

There was a lot of grunting and the sound of rocks and dirt sliding around, and I was just about to turn around when Gabriel stopped me. "No, not yet. I'll tell you when it's okay." A few more agonizing minutes later, he said, "All right now, River, you can turn around."

I turned to find a very bored-looking Gabriel standing next to a very sheepish-looking Jonas, who was wearing nothing but a pair of pants and a blush across his pale cheeks. His hair looked even more blond with his skin flushed red up to the roots, deepening in color the longer I looked. Fully clothed Jonas was a large handsome man. Half-dressed he was sinful perfection, and I forgot Gabriel was even standing there as I took in the sight of Jonas, not dead at the bottom of the cliff, but alive and in front of me.

I took three seconds to cross the distance between us and throw myself into his arms.

"You scared me today," he said, and his voice was normal and smooth again, not the deep rasp of his stone self.

"I was terrified, too," I whispered, while I rained kisses across his forehead, cheeks, and finally his lips, a light peppering of thanks for coming to my rescue. And for not perishing when I pushed him into a fifty-foot drop.

"I wasn't scared at all, if anyone cares," Gabriel drawled from next to us, reminding us we weren't alone.

"Where is Wesa?" I couldn't believe I had forgotten about him. Had he run off? Was he still hell-bent on terrorizing the people of the town if I didn't bend to his will?

"Oh, he's fine where he is." Gabriel walked over to Wesa's still form in the grass. He lay in a crumpled pile, where I assumed he'd landed when Jonas tossed him through the air.

"He's a bad man."

"He's just a human," Gabriel said, nudging Wesa's backside with the toe of his expensive shoe. "But his heart was filled with enough malice to cause irreparable damage, that's for sure. His mind was a grotesque thing, and I know the real bogeyman." Gabriel was unaffected by everything that had gone down, and as I studied him, I noticed the chain still dangling from his hand. He saw me looking and opened his fist to show me a large black stone in the center of his palm. Well, it looked black at first glance, but inside the light danced and played as if inside an ember burned.

"Sorry, my dear, no take-backs."

"I don't understand," I said, for what seemed like the hundredth time. I looked over at Jonas for clarification.

"I've done something, River," Jonas told me. "I was desperate, and you'll be angry, but I don't regret it, and it can't be undone, so even if you never want to see me again, I'd do it again in a heartbeat." He looked at me defiantly, but when I said nothing to challenge him, he continued. "River, your power is gone. I took it. We took it from you."

What? That couldn't be true. I reached down deep and tried to pull a flame—nothing. Not that I had much practice calling the fire on purpose, but still, that place that had always been bubbling inside me, just waiting for a chance to escape? That was gone. Inside me was just a quiet peaceful serenity. A calm.

"Also, just so you know, there was a bit of a wager made, and to the victor go the spoils," Gabriel interrupted, swinging the chain in his hand like a pendulum. "But in this instance, even though you are the victor, the spoils go to me."

"Gabriel, you're being obtuse," Jonas warned.

"No, I'm being honest. Your power is gone, River. I hold it here in this stone, and the stone belongs to me. Your power is now mine."

"Dammit, Gabriel . . ."

"You mean it?" The words came out on a shallow joyous breath.

"What?" the two men said in unison.

"You mean it's gone? Forever? As in no more spontaneous eruptions? No chance of me hurting anyone by accident or choice? No emotional outburst will cause me to light someone on fire?" I side-eyed Jonas as I asked the last question.

"Not a chance, my dear. You are an empty tank, so to speak, forever more."

"Oh, thank the gods," I cried, and as the tears rained down, I threw myself into Jonas's arms once again. "Let's test it. Kiss me, Jonas."

And so he did.

For so long and with so much enthusiasm that when I next came up for air, the sun had sunk low behind the trees. There was no sign of Gabriel Doyle anymore, nor was there any sign of Wesa. I had a hard time believing the dapperly dressed vampire of the Lilith Nest had dragged that sorry human down the mountainside by the shoe, but with that vampire, anything was possible.

"Jonas," I asked, turning to face him once again and caressing the side of his face. No longer was I afraid to touch him lest I singe off something important. "What do I do now?"

"I think you should continue to do the same things you have always done," he said as he grabbed my hand and we picked our way back down the path. It was much wider than I remembered on the way up, and there were downed trees all along the path, like a huge storm had whipped right up the mountain. "After all, that's the River I fell in love with."

My blush burned hot, and I could only hope I was saved from him seeing it by the dimming of the evening light. He would not let me turn away, though, and he pulled my hand until I stumbled into him. And as he pressed my small soft body against his larger, harder frame, he whispered in my ear.

"I just ask that whatever you decide to do, it's by my side, River. No more running."

I wholeheartedly agreed. "No more running."

EPILOGUE

RIVER

I don't know why Jonas ever hid his other form from me. He had said it was because he was so grotesque he didn't want to scare me, but he looked no different to me when he changed. Just much bigger . . . and harder.

To say there was a large mess to clean up would be an understatement. I knew the Court of the Sun and the Moon had a lot to do with what went on in town, but this would have been a cover-up of massive proportions. There was no way to hide what had happened, and I would have to deal with the consequences of my actions.

And I had ample time, considering I was dragged in front of the Court again, much like I had been as a child. They looked, tested, and read my mind until it satisfied them, but there was not even a minute trace of the flames left inside my body. They were well and truly gone.

And so was Wesa.

I don't mean he left town; I mean he was gone. Like he never existed. There wasn't even a whisper of a new teacher that had come into town. It was as if he had never been there in the first place. I couldn't get any information from Elsmed or any of the other members of the Court. And I would not ask Roman Bishop, who'd taken over the Court seat in his father's place. That entire family scared the hell out of me.

I'd gotten over my fear of Gabriel Doyle. Well, mostly. He was a lot easier to deal with now he'd gotten something he wanted from me, and at the very least, I was more comfortable peppering him with questions about what happened to Wesa than anyone else. After all, Gabriel could read minds, so surely he could glean that tiny bit of information.

But all I'd gotten out of Gabriel was something about sirens and the name Alverson. I didn't know what a siren was, but even Gabriel had looked uncomfortable talking about it. I might not have known a lot about the histories of other supernaturals, but I still knew enough not to pry into something that made even a vampire nervous. Wesa was gone—that was a fact. And with him went the hate, the trauma, and the violence he brought with him.

Jonas told me that Hank Weisman's memory was wiped before he left town. I didn't ask what story they gave him to replace his memory of having been in Havenwood Falls. I didn't care. It was best I let that memory leave in peace. Hopefully, the court had done a small kindness and wiped away his memory of me as well, but I couldn't ask such things.

It seemed Jonas had made a deal with Gabriel to drain my power, and as possession was nine-tenths of the law, it belonged to Gabriel now. I should have been angry, but I wasn't. I could only feel sharp relief and gratitude. It was one of those situations where the ends justified the means, even if Meri and Alice harrumphed about it. They claimed he would do something nefarious with the amulet and were shocked that the Court let him keep it. I wasn't shocked, because I was pretty sure he worked something out with Roman Bishop, since those two spoke the same language of greed. I guessed he'd just hold on to it until he could sell it to the highest bidder. Maybe Roman would be involved in that, too. Regardless, it was better off in his hands than my body, of that I was sure. I couldn't find it in me to be upset about it at all.

And now, a solid year later, summer was in full swing again. I still worked with the sisters occasionally, but I did things differently. I made the lunches and catering orders out of the home I shared with Jonas since we were married in the spring. We bought our fruits from the sisters, whose only labor now was to tend their orchards lovingly, and Jonas made me promise to drive his truck instead of my motorbike from now on.

"It isn't good for the baby," he said.

I think I'll let him have his way this once.

~

Want to read about Jonas and River's descendent? Look for *Chase the Flames* by Desiree Lafawn.

We hope you enjoyed this story in the Legends of Havenwood Falls series featuring a variety of supernatural creatures. The series is a collaborative effort by multiple authors.

Books in the historical Legends of Havenwood Falls series:

Lost in Time by Tish Thawer
Dawn of the Witch Hunters by Morgan Wylie
Redemption's End by Eric R. Asher
Trapped Within a Wish by Brynn Myers
Blood and Damnation by Belinda Boring
Fated Beginnings by E.J. Fechenda
Emeline by Katie M. John
Released From a Curse by Brynn Myers
A Pack of Lies by Kallie Ross
Kiss the Ashes by Desiree Lafawn
Hidden Truths by Colleen Nye
Wrath and Retribution by Belinda Boring
Changing Fate by Char Webster
Rise of the Witch Hunters by Morgan Wylie
The Drowning Bride by Seven Jane

Also try the main Havenwood Falls series; the YA line, Havenwood Falls High; the darker, sexier side of town, Havenwood Falls Sin & Silk; and the local supernatural college, Sun & Moon Academy.

Stay up to date at www.HavenwoodFalls.com

Subscribe to our reader group and receive free stories and more!

ABOUT THE AUTHOR

Desiree lives in Northwest Ohio with her husband, children, and two rowdy cats. She is a multi-genre author who writes contemporary romance and romantic suspense as well as paranormal romance. She's a craft-addicted amateur foodie who loves wine and snacks. Mostly snacks. In her free time, Desiree enjoys living in suburbia and being a typical soccer mom—a soccer mom who makes up amazing stories and watches a lot of anime.

Desiree can be found at her website https://desireelafawn.com/
Or on social media:
Twitter https://twitter.com/DesireeLafawn
Facebook https://www.facebook.com/DesireeLafawnAuthor/
Instagram https://www.instagram.com/desireelafawn/

ACKNOWLEDGMENTS

There are so many people to thank I don't even know where to begin. Kristie Cook and all of the collaborating authors of Havenwood Falls, thank you for letting in this little contemporary author. I'm rough around the edges and oftentimes a misfit. Thank you for opening the wards and letting me in.

E.J. Fechenda, Randi Cooley Wilson, and Victoria Flynn, thank you for sharing your characters with me. Victoria, our early morning and late night messages helped me in ways words can't describe. This book was different than anything I've written before, and you helped alleviate my fears and general curling up in a corner in the fetal position.

Thank you to the editing team for not chopping my fingers off for inappropriate comma use. I would love to promise you that I will do better in the future, but we all know better, don't we?

Regina Wamba, I am so blessed to have your designs grace my cover. I'm a lucky little author to be participating in something so huge, so amazing, so *bright*.

And readers, especially those of you who have been with this group since the very beginning, thank you for your support. You are the reason we write the words. I look forward to my future with you and the rest of Havenwood Falls.

AN EXCERPT

~ A Legends of Havenwood Falls Novella ~

HAVENWOOD FALLS LEGENDS

HIDDEN TRUTHS

COLLEEN NYE

Hidden Truths (A Legends of Havenwood Falls Novella) by Colleen Nye

A Japanese kitsune shifter discovers family secrets and hidden truths halfway around the world. She only wanted to find love.

For her more than five hundred years, kitsune Kaori Ishida has never strayed from her beloved homeland of Japan or her family. But when she falls for an American and sees hope of a normal life, she embarks on a journey to the United States. She leaves everything she knows behind, including her familiar appearance, to follow love.

Only, what she finds isn't what she expects.

With the Immigration Act of 1924 only two years old, she discovers a scary new world that doesn't accept either of her true forms. Seeking refuge and following a trail of lies, she ends up in a strange little town in the Colorado mountains, where family secrets and deceptions have her struggling to find the truth—and find herself.

HIDDEN TRUTHS

BY COLLEEN NYE

"This is foolish, Kaori. I simply do not understand." An elderly woman in a kimono held a cup of tea, the lines on her face deep with worry.

"You do not have to understand, *Okaasan*. I'm just grateful for all you've done for me—teaching me more English, helping me get my new clothes, and arranging my passage to the Americas. Not to mention always being home for me in a world I have never felt at home in." Kaori bowed slightly before embracing her mother.

Pulling back and looking over her daughter's expression, Kaori's mother sighed. "It is foolish to travel around the world for a *kareshi*."

"He's more than a boyfriend, *Okaasan*. I plan to marry him. To make him my *shujin*."

Her mother set her tea down and gripped Kaori's hands. "*Watashi no musume.* You are *nobody's* property. Never let anyone be your master."

Kaori chuckled. "I simply meant husband. Even in today's world, in the modern times of the 1920s, we women still want husbands. And he wants me as his wife. I know it. Besides, you know that no matter how much I love our family, I have never felt like I belong."

The older woman nodded slowly. "I know. And I did hear his proposal. But any man who would leave his love to go to the other side of the world, saying goodbye and leaving all that matters behind for money alone, is not honorable."

Kaori's brows furrowed. "*Okaasan*, these are different times than we come from. When will you see this?"

Her mother dropped her hands almost as fast as her expression. "Honor should not have an expiration date in society, *shin'ainaru-kun e.*"

Kaori lifted her hands again. "It's not a matter of honor as much as it is a matter of necessity and laws. Laws of many have changed our world, *Okaasan*. I am not allowed in the States as is. The recent immigration acts prohibit all Asians from entering American soil. Many of our people over there are in camps right now, simply for being of Asian descent. He could not take me with him when his employer wrote for his return because of the risks."

"Then how can you go now?"

"I shall assume a different face and body. We are kitsune. We have this power." Kaori smiled proudly.

"Why didn't you just do this and go with him then? Why wait and travel alone?" Her mother pulled away and lifted the tea once more.

Kaori put a hand on her mother's shoulder. "He does not know what we are. Not yet. But he will, once I explain. I feel it in my soul, *Okaasan*. I need to go."

"Do what you must, but know that I will not rest well without hearing from you. So visit my dreams often. *Kudasai.*" The elder hugged her daughter. "It's been over five hundred years since your birth, and we have never been more than a village away from one another."

"*Okaasan*, you can feel me wherever I am. You can hear the world."

Her mother kissed her forehead. "But I will want to *see* you. Not just spy."

Kaori's eyes filled with tears. "*Watashi wa, anata o aishiteimasu.*"

"I love you, too, Kaori."

Picking up her bags, Kaori gave her mother one last hug, made her way down to the harbor, and boarded the ship to America an Asian woman.

~

Kaori stepped onto American soil in the state of California with the appearance of a slender, attractive, brunette Englishwoman. Her dress was a bit more formal, with the new style slip dress topped with a jacket instead of the commonly seen shawl or stole. She figured, with the exhaustion and stress of the journey, she would need the extra layers to help hide her tails, which liked to slip out when she wasn't keeping them hidden.

Stepping down onto the dock, she pulled out documents from her shoulder bag and presented them as she took in the scenery. Thanks to her contacts in Japan, her paperwork was flawless. However, she worked to say as little as possible, considering that she hadn't had much practice with her accent. As much as she looked of European descent, she wasn't ready to chance anyone's reaction to her having a fluent Japanese accent, despite having just sailed from there.

Refraining from her engrained ritual of bowing when greeting someone, she simply gave a sweet smile. "Hello, sir."

After a brief moment as he looked over her documents, she was granted entrance. "Everything looks good, Miss Ipsley." He handed her back the documents. "Welcome home."

She folded the pages and put them back in her bag. "Katherine or Kay is fine." She tried on her new name.

He tipped his hat. "Have a wonderful day, Miss Ipsley."

"Thank you. You as well." She smiled.

American dollars in hand, Kaori paid a young man on the dock to help her with her trunk and find her a car to a local hotel. It didn't take her even twenty-four hours to plan a route, pay for tickets, and be on her way to Colorado. As eager as she was, she didn't want to waste any time. She boarded a train as early as she could and was on her way to Warren.

~

"Havenwood Falls, please." Kaori rested her hands on the sill of the ticket window at the train station in Grand Junction, Colorado. "The station in California said they only had tickets for trains to here and to ask once I arrived about getting closer."

The man behind the counter quirked an eyebrow. "I'm sorry, ma'am. Where did you say?"

She cleared her throat and repeated herself. "Havenwood Falls, please."

His brows furrowed at her question. "I'm sorry, miss. I'm not sure we have a train to that town. Is it in Colorado or another state?" He was flipping through a small stack of papers that listed all of the towns the trains went to. "Is it newly established?"

Kaori's heart thudded as her mind raced. She wasn't sure if she'd gotten the name of the town wrong or if she'd purposefully been given the wrong name. Either way, all she knew was that she was standing in a train station in the middle of a foreign country, completely unsure of where to go. Panic rose in her throat, and she fought to keep the guise of her appearance and not to turn into her true fox form and run out of there and all the way back to Japan.

Before she could speak, a tall, dark-haired man stepped up. He loomed over her with his stature, not just in height but build as well. "No trains go up there, but I am going that way, ma'am. You're welcome to ride along." He nodded to the older man behind the counter. "Hello, Fred."

She looked the man over before glancing back at the employee behind the booth, who had moved on to other tasks after nodding in return to being greeted. She was well aware that a human woman should be intimidated or even frightened about going off with some random stranger, especially one his size. It was dangerous even for her. But Kaori wasn't human, and she often had to remind herself of proper reactions to keep up appearances. So she put on a slight show of hesitation. "Alone? Are you um . . ."

He put a hand on her shoulder. "You are safe with me." Dropping his hand, he pulled his coat on. "My name is Theodore Brooks. Or Theo for short. I run a lumber company. I was just dropping my sister off. She was heading home after visiting for holiday."

Adjusting her shoulder bag, she reached a hand out. "Kaor—Katherine. Katherine Ipsley or Kay. Sorry. Either is fine."

He took her hand, much more gently than she expected. "Miss Ipsley, do you have luggage I can assist with?"

Giving up the façade, seeing he wasn't looking for her to be the damsel in distress just so he could pretend to be her knight in shining armor, Kaori motioned to her trunk as she lifted her handbag. "Just this. Thank you."

He gripped the handle and waved his hand for her to go ahead of him. "I'm parked just outside."

The pair stepped out into the brisk Colorado air. Theo opened the passenger door for her before pulling the trunk onto the rear of his truck and securing it with a rope. The entire vehicle jostled as he climbed in behind the wheel, reminding her of his size. But when he gave her a shy smile as he started the engine, she returned the smile and smoothed out her skirts.

After a few twists and turns on the mountain roads and many miles, Theo broke the silence. "Meeting someone?"

"Yes, I am," she replied, staring out over the landscape, still attempting to hide her lack of fluency in the American accent.

"Figures. Nobody comes to Havenwood Falls without a reason." The truck growled as he downshifted. "I won't pry."

She snapped her full attention to him. "I'm so sorry. I didn't mean to be rude."

"You're not being rude at all. It is none of my business." Theo pulled the wheel to steer them around a sharp corner.

Kaori took a breath and sat up straight, figuring this was as good a time as any to practice not only speaking but her story as well. "I've been away, and I picked up a bit of an accent, so I am shy about speaking still. Especially with the laws in effect."

"Your accent is barely noticeable." His eyes didn't leave the road.

"Thank you." Her gaze returned to the mountainside. "The

gentleman I was planning to marry was called back here sooner than expected, and I am just coming to join him."

He nodded as she spoke. "Oh? In Havenwood Falls? Really? What is his name?"

"Mr. Warren Bennet." She blushed. "He's a bookkeeper."

Sitting upright at Warren's name, Theo's posture became a bit more rigid. He appeared thankful that she was distracted by the view so he could regain his composure. "Ah, yes. Warren. Would you like me to deliver you and your luggage to his home or to your lodgings?"

"You know him?" She turned back, surprised.

"Everyone knows everyone in Havenwood Falls, miss." He turned them around another sharp curve and pulled onto County Road 13.

"Ah yes. I see." She bit her lip. "Since I don't have a room settled as of yet, if you know where he lives, I would love to surprise him. He's not expecting me."

"Oh. No doubt he isn't." Theo chuckled.

Find *Hidden Truths* where books are sold.